Final Passage

FINAL PASSAGE

Final Passage

Mystery on the Alaska Ferry

DAN PEDERSEN

Also by the Author

*

Final Deception: *A Whidbey Island Mystery*

Louis and Fanny: *15 Years on the Alaska Frontier*

Outdoorsy Male: *Short Stories and Essays*

Wild Whidbey: *The Nature of Island Life*

Whidbey Island's Special Places

R1

Front Cover: Inside Passage photographed by Dan Pedersen

ISBN: 1548204536
ISBN-13: 978-1548204532

DAN PEDERSEN

DEDICATION

For Louis and Fanny Pedersen, Alaska pioneers.

FINAL PASSAGE

ACKNOWLEDGMENTS

Thank you to the friends who read my first mystery, *Final Deception*, and encouraged me to keep the story alive in this sequel. Journalist Brad Haraldsen is back again, this time with his wife Irene and Detective Shane Lindstrom, and Alaskans Robert Yuka and Marie Martin.

My wife, Sue Van Etten, contributed the sketches. Sue has shared several Alaska adventures with me including a memorable trip on the *MV Matanuska* with Raincoat Man and the Bikers, the Dutch kid, the Californians, the Mushers and some other intriguing characters who kept us guessing.

My long-time artist friend Kris Wiltse drew the location maps. Kris has been my partner for years developing marine interpretive signage for Island County. Over the months of writing, my colleagues in the Vicious Circle writers group helped sharpen the story. They are Candace Allen, JoAnn Kane, Chris Spencer, Regina Hugo and Dave Anderson. Claire Creighton and Jim Lougy helped me find many errors my eye had overlooked, thank goodness!

I am especially grateful for the support of the Whidbey Island librarians in Oak Harbor, Coupeville, Freeland, Langley and Clinton, and the island booksellers who have become good friends. This includes Josh Hauser and Nancy Welles of Moonraker Books in Langley, Karl and Ruth King of Kingfisher Books in Coupeville, and Karen Mueller and her predecessor Diane Sullivan, of Wind & Tide Books in Oak Harbor.

FINAL PASSAGE

AUTHOR'S NOTE

In 1914 the Methodist minister in Seward, Alaska, gave his wife Fanny an ivory napkin ring as a 25th anniversary gift. It was carved by an Alaska native in Dutch Harbor from the tusk of a Pacific Walrus that died a century ago. The napkin ring, which now resides in the Seward Museum, has long intrigued me.

The preacher, Louis H. Pedersen, was my grandfather.

Louis enlisted a family friend, Captain C.B. McMullen of the coastal mail steamer, *Dora*, to procure the napkin ring for him and bring it to Seward. Louis and Fanny both sailed on McMullen's ship and he was a guest in their home and their church. I have a photograph of Fanny at the rail as the ship pulled away from Seward, which is dusted in ash from the cataclysmic eruption of Mt. Katmai.

For centuries, people all over the world have treasured ivory for its beauty and durability. Americans, British and Russians alike have long exploited Alaska and its native peoples for profit – at various times otter furs, gold, oil, animal trophies and even ivory.

And there's always some new way to make a shady dollar.

FINAL PASSAGE

Contents

Map by Kris Wiltse

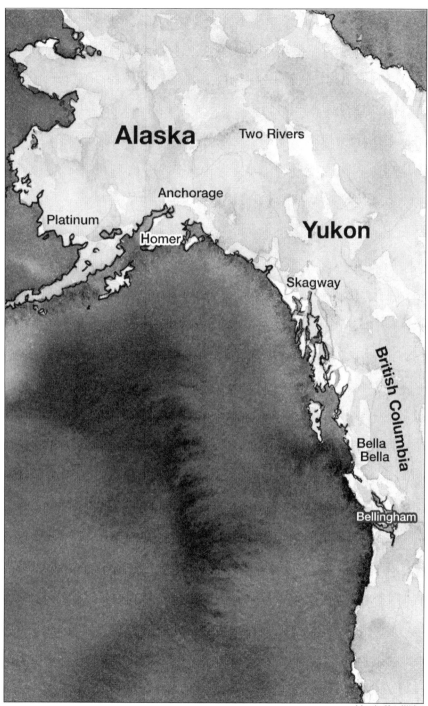

Map by Kris Wiltse

FINAL PASSAGE

Chapter 1
Bellingham

Fifty miles north of Prince Rupert, British Columbia, in the open waters of Dixon Entrance, Bob Harlowe goes over the rail. He pops to the surface briefly, shouting and waving at the disappearing ship from its frothy wake, but in the darkness it is futile. No one hears his pathetic cries over the throb of the engines. Moments later, numbed by the cold and weighted by his shoes, he slips below.

One Night Earlier

Brad Haraldsen sits up in his bunk and wonders how long he has slept since Bellingham. The hull's vibration is hypnotic, but a loose strip of molding rattles overhead. Brad has slept hard for several hours, lulled by the comforting rhythm since the Alaska Ferry *Matanuska* started its weekly run north. But he isn't sleepy now.

He reaches down to the floor and rifles through his bag. Finding what he wants, he tears a page from yesterday's *Bellingham Herald*, folds it into a wad and stuffs it into the crack over the window. The rattle stops.

Where are we? He wonders. Is it morning? Light floods through the stateroom curtains. He pulls them aside to behold a full moon rising over a mountainous silhouette to the west --Vancouver Island. The moon lights up the night like a spotlight, reflected in a broad swath across the glassy surface all the way to his window. Here and there a few scattered lights punctuate the night – houses and seaside towns, and the odd set of headlights. A brightly lit ship crosses their stern, likely the *Queen of Something,* a British Columbia ferry headed for Nanaimo.

The night is beautiful and the adventure is beginning. The hours are too precious to waste on sleep.

Brad listens to his wife, Irene, breathe soundly in the adjoining bunk. She seems happy since they stepped onto the boat, smiling and laughing, the happiest he's seen her in years. She loves an adventure and he promises her one on this trip. They'll see how others live, talk to the natives, maybe visit some Alaska dog kennels – she loves dogs – and imagine life far from their Idaho ranch.

A year earlier their marriage is all but dead. Numbed by a car accident that kills her best friend Amy, Irene retreats into wine and depression, sleeping late and wandering the house all day in her bathrobe. At the worst possible time for their marriage, Brad discovers news of his college sweetheart's death, fellow journalist Bella Morelli. Consumed by this development, Brad leaves for Whidbey Island to investigate with his best friend, Stu Wood. Stu does not return from that trip. Diagnosed with leukemia and dragged down by lifelong depression, he commits suicide on the way home, diving his airplane steeply into Washington's Lake Chelan.

It's an awful year. But free of the past, Brad turns his focus where it should have been all along, to his wife. This year becomes one of the best of their lives.

In their mid-60s, with good health, they can still dream – tackle one last adventure together while they are young enough. This is a week to take stock and reset their lives, a complete getaway from the routine of their Idaho ranch. It is also a week to be together, something they need as they rebuild a marriage coming back from a dark place.

Brad knows Irene is looking forward to sketching on this trip – her new passion. She is good, Brad thinks – can really capture the feeling of a subject in just a few lines. "You can sketch all you like this whole week," he tells her. This is your week to indulge."

It is two years since Bella's death and Brad's blockbuster expose of Whidbey Island political, economic and military collusion that drives her murderers from public office. It is the best he can do to make them pay without hard evidence to convict them in court. Brad remains certain Bella's fall from Deception Pass Bridge is murder, and County Commissioner Dorothy DeGroot and Oak Harbor Mayor Dutch DeGroot are the people who did it.

The DeGroots stake their personal wealth on Oak Harbor's booming real estate market, which is driven by ongoing Navy expansion at NAS Whidbey, and they amass political power with unwavering support of the Navy's plans. Dorothy is well positioned to run for Congress when the incumbent retires, but Brad's expose in the *Washington Post* puts an end to those dreams. Their real estate empire deflates as the Navy cuts back. Speculation is rampant in the community about their role in Bella's death. Dutch is discredited and then defeated for reelection as Oak Harbor's mayor.

The hard-hitting *Post* story is a departure from Brad's usual work. It is more in the tradition of Bella's fearless style of journalism. After graduation from the University of Washington, Brad gravitates toward human interest and he rises to national prominence as a National Public Radio contributor specializing in stories of everyday people doing positive things in their communities.

In the two years since writing the Whidbey story, Brad turns his attention solely to rebuilding his troubled marriage. Free of Bella's recurring presence in his life, his efforts pay off and this vacation is the crowning step. He feels optimistic.

Brad knows they will be underway two days on this first leg in the Inside Passage, mostly in Canadian waters, before they reach Alaska and the *Matanuska's* first stop in Ketchikan, followed soon after by additional stops in Wrangell, Petersburg, Juneau, Haines and Skagway. Then they'll start back to Bellingham via an additional stop in Sitka. For walk-ons like himself and Irene, there is plenty of time to read a book, make some new friends, savor the rugged sights and do some quick shore excursions.

He rises quietly and slips into his jeans and a sweatshirt, pushes open the heavy door and steps into the hall. He holds onto the door till it latches behind him with a click, then heads down the corridor toward the stern.

The cafeteria is deserted – nearly so – but there will be coffee in the self-service urns. As a writer this is what he loves – the stillness of the night. It is his best hour.

Friends recommend this April sailing so Brad and Irene may enjoy the preseason, when the pace on the ferry is laid back, free of summer crowds, yet with the real possibility of lovely weather on the Inside Passage. The purser tells him there are just 123 passengers on this Bellingham-to-Ketchikan leg, maybe a quarter of the boat's capacity.

Brad has read a bit of the *Matanuska's* history. Built in 1963, a year after the Seattle World's Fair, it is one of the older vessels in the system's fleet. In the summertime the Bellingham to Skagway run belongs to the larger and newer flagship, *MV Columbia,* serving huge summer crowds. In the off season the ferries operate usually with lighter loads and smaller vessels.

What startles many people is that in 1978, the *Matanuska* went back to the shipyard to be stretched 58 feet. Workers cut it in half and added a new section in the middle to increase its capacity.

Brad enters the gleaming cafeteria and fills a cup with black coffee. He has the place to himself except for one other figure, a man in a black hoodie at a table across the room, hunched over a book. He must be a fellow insomniac, but the man's body language rings a bell. Is he imagining this?

Brad crosses the room, hesitates, then speaks almost apologetically: "Shane?"

The man looks up from his book, his expression at first confused, then breaks into a broad grin. "Brad? What the *hell* are you doing here?" he asks, pushing back his chair to stand, and pumping his hand in a firm shake. "You're the last person on earth I expected to see. Besides, it is 2:30 a.m."

"Yeah, I know," Brad replies. "Normal people sleep. Which begs the question, what the hell are *you* doing here – at this hour?"

"Well for one thing I'm trying to keep a low profile."

Two years earlier, Shane Lindstrom and Brad worked together to find the truth behind the mysterious death of journalist Bella Morelli. Bella's body was found in the waters east of Deception Pass Bridge on Whidbey Island, with injuries that suggested a suicide jump. Brad never believed she jumped. Shane was the lead investigator for the Island County Sheriff's Department at that time and he didn't buy it either. Brad soon realized Shane was another of Bella's friends, maybe a little more.

"What are you doing here?" Shane asks.

"I'm on vacation with Irene, taking the boat to Skagway and back. Is your wife on the boat, too?"

"No," Shane replies. "We don't spend much time together. We're separated and Billy lives with her. The sheriff let me go right after the newspaper article. By the way, thank you for that – sincerely. Judy stayed in Coupeville and I moved to Bellingham. I'm with the Whatcom County Sheriff now. Technically, this week I'm on a little solo vacation."

"Technically," Brad repeats, with a knowing wink.

"Technically. It's a bit of personal unfinished business, keeping a friendly eye on some old friends of ours."

Brad's mind races. "You can't possibly mean who I think you mean."

"They're on this boat."

Two years earlier Dorothy and Dutch DeGroot are Island County's preeminent power couple – she a county commissioner and he the mayor of Oak Harbor. They are the island's foremost real estate developers and loudest cheerleaders for the Navy's insanely noisy Growler aircraft.

More to the point, Brad and Shane are pretty sure the DeGroots murdered Bella Morelli by throwing her off Deception Pass Bridge and claiming it was suicide.

"Do you mind?" Brad asks, nodding at the chair across from Shane. He puts down his cup, pulls out the chair, and sits down. He takes a slow sip, looks up and asks, "So how are things going for the DeGroots these days?"

"Well, as you know, your *Washington Post* article about Bella's death and the links to the DeGroots and the Navy triggered all kinds of mayhem. The Navy launched a full-scale review and put a freeze on expanded Growler operations at NAS Whidbey. Real estate development on north Whidbey went into a tailspin and the DeGroots found themselves up to their armpits in financial quicksand."

"Gosh I can't say I'm sorry," Brad remarks. "They should both be behind bars."

"Working on that," Shane notes. "There's been a certain pleasure in watching them scurry for cover like cockroaches."

"So what are they up to now?"

"Well, they actually shifted assets into a new company, DeGroot Air. On the surface it seems benign enough, running charter flights, guided hunts and taxi service to wilderness camps, and transporting air freight to various Alaska communities and points in the bush. Some of their flights operate out of Bellingham Airport, which kinda gives me an excuse to keep my toe in the water."

He continues, "The thing is, if a pilot is willing to look the other way now and then, he can charge a premium to transport illegal cargo and fly trophy hunters to remote camps for un-permitted hunts. Most pilots and guides don't want any part of that. So that leaves a niche for an outfit that's willing to play loose with the rules, such as DeGroot Air. In fact I'd say the DeGroots have institutionalized this."

"Isn't an airline way outside their comfort zone?" Brad asks. "What do they know about that?"

"You might think so, but in all those years of promoting the Navy, Dutch made a lot of relationships in the aviation community. And there is money to be made in Alaska especially – quite a shortage of pilots these days. Per capita, the state needs six times as many pilots as the rest of the country. Alaska has always drawn young pilots from the Lower 48, but the Baby Boom generation is retiring. There's a huge demand for a new company like DeGroot Air and the pilots it can recruit."

"So given all that, Shane, why are you wasting your time following the DeGroots around on the Alaska Ferry?"

"Because I received an anonymous tip. And I still want to lock them up."

Chapter 2
BC Sunshine Coast

Irene Haraldsen wakes alone, with a hearty appetite for breakfast. She isn't surprised Brad has already gotten up and gone searching for coffee.

Like any good Idaho girl she has a craving for bacon and eggs. Waking up on a boat to Alaska just throws fuel on that fire. Oatmeal would be the sensible choice but she's on vacation. This isn't the time to be sensible. She is pretty sure she'll find Brad in the cafeteria anyway.

According to her iPhone it is just 5 a.m., which is 4 a.m. ship's time. Once you step aboard you're on Alaska time for the whole trip, the purser tells her. Back home in Idaho this is 6 a.m. Mountain Time. She hasn't risen this early in years. She misses her dogs and horses, but they are in good hands for the week with a cowboy named Bolivar, the Basque foreman of their ranch.

Irene's girlfriends in her Stanley, Idaho, book club urge her to go for broke on this second honeymoon and insist on a luxury cruise. Brad convinces her that to meet real Alaskans they should travel with the unwashed masses on the blue canoe, as Alaskans call the blue-hulled state ferries. This particular run, the only one that connects to Bellingham in the Lower 48, is called the mainline.

Secretly, the ferry is more her style than a cruise ship anyway. It suits her adventurous spirit. She splashes water in her face and looks at the tiny shower. Really? A human body fits in that space? She'll deal with it later. She slips into a Redfish Lake sweatshirt and jeans, and runs a comb through her shoulder-length hair. Good enough for this early. At 6-foot-1, with raven hair and a young woman's figure, she can still turn a few heads. She won't meet anyone she knows on this boat anyway.

Sunrise is still an hour away but the eastern horizon is filling with color. She steps out on deck for some air and takes a swing through the forward observation lounge for a better look at the dawn before heading to the cafeteria.

*

She finds Brad right where she expects – drinking coffee at a table in the far corner of the cafeteria. He has already made a friend, it appears. She pours a cup of coffee and heads across the room. He is so deep in conversation he does not even look up till she sets her saucer next to his.

"Oh, good morning honey," Brad greets. "Pull up a chair. I ran headlong into my friend Shane," he tells her, then turns to Shane and announces, "my wife, Irene."

"Shane?" Irene repeats. "You're not *the* Shane, are you, the Whidbey Island detective?"

"Used to be," Shane replies. "I'm with Whatcom County now."

Brad jumps in. "Shane has been filling me in on what happened since the article came out two years ago. Apparently this boat trip is going to be a lot more interesting than we expected because our chief suspects in the murder are aboard."

"Wait a minute," Irene says, rolling her eyes. "This is beyond coincidence. Did you know this when we signed up?"

"I swear I didn't," Brad replies, looking her right in the eyes. "Shane is the last person I expected to see, and he's only here because the DeGroots are here."

"It's true," Shane interrupts. "And I'm really sorry if this screws up your vacation."

"No, no, no. Not at all," Irene replies, reaching across and placing her hand on the back of Shane's hand. "This ramps up the adventure nicely. Tell me what's going on."

Shane and Brad lay out the situation. An Oak Harbor man identifying himself as a pilot for DeGroot Air calls Shane a week ago to say his bosses are up to something illegal that violates his conscience. He will not give his name, but says he is giving Shane this tip because of his role in the Whidbey Island investigation two years ago.

"So what does this boat have to do with any of it?" Irene asks.

"The caller said the DeGroots and several of their employees are taking the ferry to Skagway and back under the cover of tourism, but actually holding meetings on board and transporting some prohibited cargo back to Bellingham. He wasn't sure about the cargo but it was clear that his job as a pilot would be to fly some loads from point to point and be discrete about it, and not ask any questions."

"This is big," Brad says. "Any idea how many of their people are on this boat?"

"Not a clue," Shane replies. "At least several. It's a light passenger load so that's going to make it easier for us. I alerted the purser and captain that I'm aboard and keeping an eye on some people."

"But once Dot and Dutch know we are on the boat, they're going to go deep and stay there," Brad says.

"That's a problem," Shane agrees.

Irene looks up from her coffee. "So let me help. They don't know me. I can drift around, strike up some conversations, keep my eyes and ears open."

"Are you sure?" Shane asks.

"This is perfect!" she insists. "Look, I'm going to be sketching this whole trip. That gives me an excuse to watch people, and most of them are flattered about the attention."

"Then Shane and I had better get the heck out of this cafeteria before they see us, and see you with us," Brad says. "We'll leave you to have breakfast in peace. But just remember, you don't have to do any of this, you know. Don't take any risks."

"No, I want to. You know I'm a good mingler. This is the kind of thing my friend Amy would jump all over if she were still alive. Maybe we can finish what you and Shane started."

Irene gets up and heads for the serving line. Shane pushes back his chair and walks to the exit, followed a moment later by Brad.

Chapter 3
Northbound

"I wish I had your talent," a woman's voice declares over Irene's shoulder. She turns to find a strikingly beautiful blonde, sixtyish, quite tall. Irene is just putting the finishing strokes on a pen-and-ink sketch of two long-haired, tattooed bikers in leathers who are snoring on the floor of the forward observation lounge. Their skin, what she can see of it, is covered with swastikas, iron crosses, skulls and the like.

A pigtailed, pre-teen girl who has been idly looking out the windows comes over and joins them. "You make that look easy," she remarks.

"It comes with practice. I'm still learning," Irene says. "It's my answer to knitting or doodling – something to keep my hands busy."

A handsome young boy with a backpack joins them. "I've been watching you sketch," he says. "Would you sketch me for my parents in Holland?"

"I'd be happy to."

"Obviously," the tall woman says, "I'm not alone thinking you have talent. You've really captured the faces and body language in just a few lines."

Irene turns her swivel chair to face the visitor. "I don't know. I throw away most of my sketches, but every so often I get one worth keeping. By the way I'm pleased to meet you – my name's Irene Johnson," she says, using her maiden name.

"Well I'm Dorothy DeGroot," the visitor replies.

"Vacationing?"

"Yes, up-and-back vacation for me. Business for my husband – meeting with some of his people and gearing up for the Alaska tourist season with his bush air service."

"That sounds exotic. My husband and I are just Idaho farmers," Irene says, glancing up briefly and then turning her eyes back to the sketch.

"Potatoes?" Dorothy asks. "That's what I think of when I hear Idaho – Famous Potatoes, as it says on the license plates."

"No, we grow hay and horses."

"I was a farm girl myself," Dorothy says. "Daddy had a turkey ranch on Whidbey Island but it didn't get off the ground."

"So what do you do now?" Irene asks.

"Believe it or not my husband and I drifted into politics for a few years. Now my husband is just starting up his little airline, god help us."

They both laugh. This woman is a master at putting an innocent face on what she's really up to, Irene thinks as she stares into Dorothy's eyes.

"You have a beautiful face, Dorothy, beautiful skin," Irene comments. "You don't see that every day in women our age. If you're going to be on this boat for a few days I'd love to sketch you. I'll add some watercolors later."

Dorothy blushes. "I'll be right here," she says, "languishing."

They both laugh.

"I think there will be a lot to see but we'll also have some hours to fill," Irene says. "Let's make sure we get together again."

"I'd like that," Dorothy declares. "Now I must go find some

breakfast." She turns and starts out of the lounge.

One of the bikers snorts and shifts onto his side. Irene quickly puts down her sketch pad and looks away.

"I think your subjects are waking up," says an older, crew cut man with a cane in a nearby seat, who's been watching them out of the corner of his eye. "I wouldn't start anything with those two."

"I think you're right," Irene replies. "You folks vacationing?"

"Just riding up and back, enjoying the sights."

"Well then I guess we're going to be shipmates for a while. My name's Irene Johnson."

"I'm Jack Evans and this is my wife Alta," he replies, nodding to the white-haired lady in the adjacent seat. "From California."

"Is this your first trip?"

"Oh heavens no," Jack says. "We've been to Alaska many times. We love the ferry and people watching."

Irene knows what they mean. The ship is filled with characters. She finds herself falling into the rhythm of the ship – daydreaming a bit, reading, turning inward. With each hour now they leave civilization further behind on both sides of the ship – no more BC Sunshine Coast, only isolated houses and widely scattered shoreline communities. Hours pass with trees and rocky shorelines, and the occasional navigation beacon. She guesses they must be approaching the north end of Vancouver Island where they'll make the first of two open-water crossings on this otherwise sheltered route. She is a little apprehensive about that. Will her Idaho stomach handle that?

"You should sketch that guy over there," Jack says, nodding across the room to a tall, slim, solitary figure in a black raincoat, dark glasses, black top hat and a bushy black mustache. "He's the most distinctive character we've seen so far on this trip."

"What do you make of him?" Irene asks.

"We're stumped."

Preacher? Weirdo? G-man? Assassin? Irene doesn't have a clue. But Jack is right; he's a great subject for a sketch. She'll have to do it on the sly.

Out on the deck, another guy in dark glasses sunbathes with a honey-colored Labrador at his feet. The dog wears a "Service Dog" vest. This guy looks like a local, Irene thinks.

Life in the lounge is quiet, almost reverent. The engines here are nearly silent. People read books, doze or converse in hushed tones, as if in a library or church. She gets up and drifts quietly through the sparse crowd, listening. A large, middle-aged couple, Texan she thinks, talk about repairs they'll make this summer on their remote cabin in the interior. A boat captain from Port Townsend spins stories to the couple beside him about his whale-watching tours out of Juneau. A young man who seems to be a seasonal plumber in Wrangell gives some other guy the details of his peeing problem, and enlarged prostate.

But what catches her eye is a handsome, clean-cut man in his 30s, sitting alone, reading a book. She gets up and wanders over to his side of the room, stopping behind him and looking out the window between glances his way. When he closes the book to rest his eyes she notices the title, *The Alaska Bush Pilot Chronicles.*

"Forgive me, is that any good?" she asks.

 "Well," he replies, startled. "It . . . uh, depends on your taste. I'm always picking up something new about flying."

"Like what?" Irene asks.

"Oh gosh, mostly aircraft loading, trim and such. In the bush a lot of us have to fly at the limits, at least on takeoff."

"Have you been flying up here long?"

"Just one season. Last summer I flew mostly soda pop to Eek and other Yukon Delta native communities. This summer for my new boss I'll be flying more hunters and general cargo."

"Wait a minute. There's a town named Eek?"

"Yes, and when you fly into it and see where you have to land, that's what you say. The plane has these big tundra tires that help smooth out the bumps. In the winter sometimes it's easier to just land on the river."

"Well I'm a horse rancher from Idaho so this Alaska lore is all new to me."

"Really? Whereabouts?"

"Little village of Stanley, in the mountains, right in the middle of Idaho. We even have an airstrip, probably a lot like the ones you're used to in the Alaska bush. And it snows a lot in the winter."

"Actually, ranching in Idaho sounds a little saner to me than flying into some of these remote villages in the dead of winter," the pilot laughs. "But Alaska is a good place for a Lower 48 pilot to get some hours, and there's a shortage of pilots, so we have lots of job opportunities."

"So why are you traveling on the ferry?" Irene asks. "Couldn't you get to your job a lot faster by flying?"

"Well, my plane is in Juneau and I'm riding north with my boss and some of his other employees. The boat gives us a few days to get acquainted and talk a bit. We're still ironing out some things about the job."

"Must be hard to be away from your family so much. You don't have a wife or girlfriend at home?"

"No, I'm quite on my own. My parents are no longer living so it's just me and my kid sister back in Auburn. The lack of attachments makes this work a little easier in some ways, but I don't see myself doing it for longer than a few more years."

Well I hope you get the terms you want from your boss before you reach Juneau."

"Why thank you. Me, too. In case I don't, do you have any openings for a ranch hand?"

"Let's keep in touch about that," Irene replies with a bat of the lashes. "It's a pretty ranch, with dogs and horses, and Stanley is a picture postcard village in the mountains. I think you would like it.

.

Chapter 4
Queen Charlotte Sound

A knock on Shane's cabin door rouses him and Brad from their discussion. "I thought I'd find you here," Irene says. "I brought you both takeout of sausage and eggs, and a little fruit," handing them each a paper plate covered in tin foil.

"The cafeteria let you do this?" Brad asks.

"I had to give them a cock-and-bull story about my husband throwing out his back."

"Thank goodness," Shane says. "The trouble with hiding out is that it's more of a weight-loss program than I had in mind."

"So how was your walkabout?" Brad asks.

"Productive."

"May I have your attention please," begins an announcement on the public address system in Shane's room. *"In about 40 minutes we will enter open water in Queen Charlotte Sound and experience some side-to-side rocking for about two hours. At that time we will ask you to be seated and minimize moving about for your own safety. But right now, if you have dogs or other pets in your vehicle you'd like to attend to, the car deck will be open for the next 20 minutes."*

"Sounds like we are getting to the fun part," Brad says.

Irene rolls her eyes and goes back to filling in Brad and Shane on her conversation with the very charming Dot DeGroot. "I think we're fast friends already. And also, Shane, in case you're interested, I think I found your pilot."

"I need to talk with him if I can find a way to do it privately," Shane says. "But I don't want to spook him or get him in Dutch with the DeGroots."

Brad and Irene groan in chorus.

"Do we know which cabin the DeGroots are in?" Brad asks. "We don't want to run headlong into them in the corridor."

"We're in luck on that. Purser told me they're in 32C, portside at the stern. That's a long haul from us here in 11B, starboard toward the bow. They'll be using mostly the port corridor."

"And Irene and I are near you in 13C so that's good," Brad notes. "Did you get the pilot's name?"

"I screwed up and didn't introduce myself," Irene says. "I'll get it next time I bump into him."

"What else?"

Irene tells them about the biker dudes and shows them her sketch. Also the sweet couple from California, the Texans with the backwoods cabin, the Port Townsend boat captain, the blind guy with the service dog, the Wrangell plumber who can't pee, the pre-teen girl and the Dutch kid who wants a sketch for his parents. And a very pleasant cabin steward.

She also tells them of her swing through the solarium, where the tent campers are set up on deck, and the recliner lounge. "Those are the hardcores," she says, "sleeping outside or sleeping in their chairs."

"It's a start," Brad says. "The DeGroots must have some more of their people on this boat than just the pilot."

"I think I'll hang out a bit tonight in the bar," Irene says. "A little alcohol often gets people talking and I might meet a different class of travelers."

"Keep in mind," Shane adds, "we have long stops coming up in Ketchikan, Juneau and Skagway, and shorter ones in Wrangell, Petersburg and Haines. Some passengers will leave us and others will come aboard. We've got to be on top of the changes."

Chapter 5
Platinum, Bristol Bay

One thousand miles to the west, a single-engine Cessna 172 approaches the Bering Sea coast under a low overcast. Bristol Bay typically enjoys about three clear days in May. This isn't one of them, pilot Paul Fisher muses. But he has the gravel airstrip in view. If the wind cooperates, it will be an easy landing at the unattended airstrip in Platinum, population 63.

It is still early and no one pays much notice to bush planes coming and going from the little Native village. He will unload his cargo of Coca Cola and a few groceries for the village store, pick up two hunters and their gear, and be on his way in 20 minutes.

He can see his passengers and a big pile of bags waiting in the open. There is no terminal – not even a shack. Paul circles the airstrip, sets his flaps and brings the plane down with a much wilder bounce than he intends. He taxies over to the waiting men, cuts the engine and pops the door.

"Looking for a ride to Haines?" he asks them.

"Where's the regular guy – the one who dropped us off?" one of the men shouts. "Are you with DeGroot?"

"I'm filling in," Paul replies. "The other guy is grounded with mechanical problems in Fairbanks."

"Well, you're right on time. But when I saw that bounce, partner, I thought maybe you changed your mind."

"Not what I expected to do," Paul scowls as he climbs down, opens the cargo hatch and begins offloading the Coca Cola and other cargo for the village store. "The wind is a little frisky this morning."

"We need to make some time," one of the hunters remarks as he reaches into the hold to help Paul unload. "We're meeting the ferry tomorrow in Haines."

"That shouldn't be a problem," Paul says, eyeballing the hunters' gear. "Not many hunters out this time of year."

"Special permits," the bearded guy says. "Subsistence," and they laugh.

"Platinum isn't much of a place to base yourselves," he remarks.

"We don't require a lot of luxuries," the chatty one offers, laughing again.

"That's quite a pile of bags. So what do we have here?"

"You ask a lot of questions."

"I have to balance the load."

"Rifles, tents, provisions, communications gear – that sort of stuff," the talkative one explains, lifting the first of the heavy bags and pushing it into the hold in front of the pilot.

"I can do that if you like," Paul says. "I need to get a feel for the load as I pack it."

"No you don't, pal," the hunter says. "I'm touchy about people feeling my stuff. Nothing personal."

Twenty minutes later the little plane is wheels up, wobbling in the wind as it banks away from the Bering Sea coast. Paul has a bad feeling about these guys.

"We'll refuel in Homer," Paul shouts over the engine. "I've burned some fuel getting here and Haines is a little beyond what we can do in one hop with this load."

The plane soon is just a speck over the tundra, a tiny marvel of technology in a world untouched by humans for millions of years.

In Homer, Paul will make a phone call.

Chapter 6
Bella Bella, BC

What have we gotten into? Brad wonders as he lies awake with his eyes closed. Irene naps in the adjacent bunk. After their early morning in the cafeteria with Shane, it feels good to lie down and drift with the rhythm of the ship.

This was to be a carefree getaway with Irene from the routine of their Stanley, Idaho, ranch. Now, suddenly, it is a cat-and-mouse game with the people who most likely murdered Brad's first love. He thought he had finally closed the book on that memory two years ago after he wrote the *Washington Post* expose that interrupted the Navy buildup of Growlers and brought down the DeGroot real estate empire on Whidbey Island.

Now Irene is right in the middle of it by her own choice and they could both be in danger.

The greater question is what he expects to accomplish. He is a journalist, *Idaho's Story Teller,* best known as a National Public Radio personality for positive pieces about everyday people. Crime is not his niche.

On the other hand, pure coincidence has handed him and Irene an opportunity to help put these people away. Dorothy and Dutch DeGroot do not know Irene. She can circulate around the boat, keep her eyes and ears open, and feed information to him and to Shane Lindstrom, the Bellingham detective who is dogging the DeGroots. Irene opens her eyes.

"I've been lying here wondering," she announces. "What in the world are these people up to?"

"Honestly," Brad says, sitting up and rubbing the sleep from his face, "it could be anything. Alaska attracts people who like to take shortcuts. There are plenty of ways to do that and get away with it when distances are so great and nobody's watching."

"Such as?"

"Oh, all kinds of illegal hunting and fishing, for one. You've got wolves, polar bears, grizzlies, walrus, goats, wolves. There are some rich people who collect trophies and will pay almost anything to bag one. Some of the permits are almost impossible to get. A bush airline is well positioned to move these hunters in and out of remote destinations and bring back the spoils."

"Makes sense."

"Then there's another whole layer. You've got natives and native corporations, and subsistence rights. Natives fall under some special rules, so there's the potential to make a lot of money by trading illegally."

"Well Shane suspects something or he wouldn't be on this boat," she replies.

"All I know is a guy called him and said he was a pilot for DeGroot Air, and he thinks his bosses are involved in illegal activities. He specifically said something big is going to happen on the Alaska Ferry. Obviously, the guy doesn't want his name connected to the tip in any way. That's the guy we need to find, and you're probably the best one to do that without arousing suspicions."

Brad rises and begins rummaging in his duffel bag, setting aside neatly folded shirts till he reaches a navy hooded sweatshirt toward the bottom. He explores the bag's corners with his hand and emerges with a pair of dark sunglasses. In front of the mirror, he puts on the sunglasses and then cinches up the hood around his head till just an oval of his nose, mouth and eyes is visible.

"Seriously?" Irene laughs.

"Seriously what?"

"Seriously, you're going out like that? You look ridiculous."

"I can't stay in this room forever. Nobody goes to Alaska and never leaves the room."

Brad suddenly realizes the ship's engines have quieted way down and the ride is very calm. They are still a day away from their first stop in Ketchikan, so what is this?

Pulling aside the window curtain, Irene remarks, "There's a village out here – cars and people and everything. Let's go have a look." So they head out to the rail, Brad in his hoodie and sunglasses.

"I'll keep my distance so nobody sees us together," Brad says.

"Please do."

After nearly a day of traveling through wilderness, the ship is now gliding slowly across a very still bay, leaving no wake. Motorboats speed past the ferry and across its bow. Bald eagles circle overhead.

A crew cut cabin steward in a white smock and black slacks stands at the rail smoking a cigarette and soaking up the sunshine. Brad finds a spot nearby.

"Bella Bella," the steward says, turning toward him. "Largest First Nations community on the BC coast. It'll take us a little while to get through here before we can resume speed."

"What a surreal place," Brad replies, "a world cut off from the world."

"Whole different way of life," the steward replies, stubbing out his cigarette in a nearby butt can and exhaling one last lungful of smoke. "There are several of these first nations communities tucked away on inlets and such. This is the largest. But even here, you can't get away from drugs and alcohol, and diabetes, and TV."

"Those are problems here?"

"They go where we go," the steward replies, shaking his head. "It's bad enough we nearly destroyed the native cultures with alcohol. Many communities now ban alcohol, but soda pop takes its place. My dentist does some volunteer work in remote villages and says it just breaks his heart."

Brad thinks it's ironic the steward recognizes the addictive damage of alcohol and sugar, yet indulges his own addiction to cigarettes. He changes the subject. "How do people get back and forth to these remote places?" Brad asks.

"There is some airline service. On the outer coast, the Queen Charlotte Islands are served by the BC Ferries. Actually, that's the old name. The islands were formally renamed a few years ago as the

Haida Gwaii. That's the Haida homeland – about 10,000 people."

"How much longer till Ketchikan?" Brad asks.

"We'll be there when you wake up tomorrow," the steward says. "There's a good restaurant for breakfast right across from the landing – in fact it's called The Landing. Or you can take a cab or bus downtown. It's a couple miles. You'll have about three hours of shore time."

Brad watches till most of the buildings are behind the ship, then makes his way back to the cabin, where Irene is waiting.

"Did you see that creepy guy in the black hat, black sunglasses and black raincoat?" she asks. "He looks like the angel of death. Very bizarre."

"In what way?"

"Talks to no one. Never smiles. Just stands there like he's in an altered state. I saw him in the cafeteria and lounge yesterday. Totally alone. Totally self-contained. Always dressed the same."

"Keep an eye on him," Brad urges.

"Don't worry. I'm treating everyone on this ship as a suspect. By the way, what now? I didn't see Dorothy or anyone else I recognized in the crowd when we passed Bella Bella."

"Much as I hate to encourage a bad habit," Brad replies, "you should probably hang out in the bar for a while tonight and see if you can find that pilot. The sooner we talk to him, the better."

Chapter 7
Burwash Landing, Yukon

Ten hours into a drive that starts at midnight, 20 dogs erupt into a chorus of barking and howling behind Hank Hickok's head. The truckload of Alaska Huskies feel him tap the brakes and turn the old four-wheel-drive pickup with the dog box toward a small cluster of shabby homes and drab cinder block buildings.

"Wow, civilization!" announces the teen boy in the passenger seat as he opens his eyes and sits up, pulling his earbuds free. "Where are we?"

"Welcome to the living, Trek," Hank says. "This is downtown Bur*warrsh* Landing, Yukon Territory, pop-u-lation 95," he drawls. "Good place to eat your mama's sandwiches by the lake and get these mutts out for some air."

Hank takes a left on Jimmy Joe Drive and pulls over in a clearing by the shore where they can have some privacy and space with the dogs. They have covered 432 miles since leaving Two Rivers, outside Fairbanks, with just a few pee breaks to drain the memory of a Thermos of coffee.

"What gives with this place?" Trek asks. "This is like the armpit of the earth."

"First Nations," Hank says. "Burwash is headquarters of the Kluane First Nations."

"Awesome," he replies in a sarcastic tone. "What do people do here, drink?"

"Tough place to get through the winter," Hank allows, nodding. "Highway maintenance, groceries, gas and beer, I suppose."

"How much longer to Haines?"

"Five hours if we don't blow a radiator hose and the border cops don't screw us over when we cross back into Ameracuh."

"I thought Sgt. Preston back at Beaver Creek would never let us go," Trek said.

"Mounties are always touchy about Alaskans. Minute they see Alaska plates they *know* we have guns somewhere in the vehicle. So they go through everything. It's hard enough to line up all the vet certificates and health records. Canada is a huge hassle. It's a little easier crossing back into Alaska, so I think it'll go faster at Pleasant Camp."

"Is that why you didn't want to meet those guys till we got to Haines?"

Hank smiles. "Keeping it simple, son. They're delivering some bags and we're hauling them to Juneau. It'll help out with truck expenses and ferry fare. But the last thing we need is to drag their stuff through two customs crossings if we can work around it."

"What's in the bags?" Trek asks.

"I didn't ask and they didn't tell."

Hank and Trek swing open their doors and jump down.

"Give me a hand will you son?" Hank asks, stepping around to the dog box. He opens one of the compartments and snaps a leash on the first dog. "Grab some water dishes and a bag of dogfood. Let's exercise about three at a time."

"Come on, Palin baby, you're first – this is your lucky day," he says, lifting a lean, muscular female from its compartment and setting it down.

"Dad, you don't have much more on your bones than she does."

"Well, that makes me a lean, mean machine," Hank says. "You and I may not be built for football but I garntee we are for mushing. A sled driver is just so much dead weight for the dogs to pull, so the smaller we are, the faster *they* are," he says, pointing to the dog box. "Ever wonder why so many damn women run the Iditarod? Lighter guys like us are the future of the sport."

"Now," Hank continues, "you get Bristol, Willow and Piper out of their crates, will ya? They could use some fresh air."

Chapter 8
Dixon Entrance

"So I'm barreling up the trail on the Arctic Cat, throttle wide open," a big guy with a full beard tells the bikers over beers at a corner table of the *Matanuska* bar. "I come flying around the bend and there's this 800-pound cow moose standing right in the trail, pawing the ground. 'Oh shit,' I think,'" pounding his fist. "'I am totally screwed. I got nowhere to go.'"

Irene surveys the dozen men in the *Matanuska* bar. She wouldn't mind hearing the rest of the moose story but really can't see herself at the biker table. In another corner, the black raincoat man sits alone, nursing a drink on ice cubes and staring straight ahead. This is her chance to cozy up to him, but does he even speak English? Maybe that's the problem.

Across the room, a friendly face looks up from his drink and smiles –

the bush pilot. He gestures toward an empty chair across from him and Irene gratefully accepts his invitation. She can't help feeling the smile puts a happy face on a melancholy mood.

"Interesting group here," she says, pulling back the chair.

"Flotsam and jetsam of society," the pilot says.

"Those bikers give me the creeps."

"Bulk and Sieve."

"You know their names?"

"Yeah and you're right – you don't want to know them. They're ex-cons. The night's young. I expect it will get more interesting."

The bartender in a white shirt and tie looks their way. "What'll it be, ma'am?"

"Alaskan amber," she declares, turning back to her tablemate and whispering. "Did I do that well?"

"Like a native. Enjoying the trip?" he asks.

"The scenery is beautiful – so remote. I loved Bella Bella, when we slowed down for the village. I've never sketched so fast in my life. But listen, we never got properly introduced the other day. I'm Irene Johnson," she declares, extending her hand.

"Bob Harlowe," he replies, taking her hand and wincing. "That must be an Idaho handshake."

"Yeah, I forget sometimes I'm not grabbing a horse's leg. How have you been, Bob, since we talked?"

"Struggling a bit," he says. "Nice to have some pleasant company."

Irene notices the bikers staring their way and shivers.

"I look for my boss to show up shortly and then I suppose the conversation won't be quite this pleasant. We agreed to talk here. I'll probably have to tell him I'm quitting, so I'm basically wasting this trip to Juneau."

"Can I offer you a sympathetic ear?" she asks as the bartender sets a frosty mug of beer on the table in front of her.

"I'd love it," Bob continues, "but I have to be little discrete. I've gotten myself into a situation with some people who are accustomed to having their way, and the problem now is to ease out of it gracefully. I'm not sure I can. Could I ask you to take out your sketch pad and act like you're sketching me?"

"Of course," Irene says, reaching into her purse for her pad and pen, and flipping to the first blank page. Irene leans back, makes a show of studying Bob's face for a moment, then makes a few strokes on the page.

"You know what," Bob says, "let's talk about you. Didn't you say you're with your husband on this trip?"

"Yes, this is a little getaway for us from the ranch in Stanley."

"But he's not here in the bar?" Bob says.

"He's not much for nightlife and alcohol but lets me go for this nightcap with his blessing."

"An enlightened fellow," Bob says with a chuckle.

"Good man," Irene replies, looking down at her glass and hesitating. "I think that's what keeps me with him. The last few years were a little rocky but I never doubted his honesty and integrity."

"It would be a better world if we all lived by that standard," Bob says. "And you're ranchers?"

"Well, we have a big horse ranch – my horses. He's more of an armchair cowboy. His day job is journalism. You may have heard him read his pieces on National Public Radio – Idaho's Storyteller."

"I have," Bob remarks, "and I'm impressed."

"He looks for the good in people. That's his strength – that and his sense of justice." From the corner of her eye, she notices the bikers turn back to their beers and the bearded guy with the Arctic Cat. But raincoat man just keeps staring. He needs a better name, such as the Angel of Death.

"This Idaho business isn't just a cover story, is it?" Bob asks nervously. "You aren't with the police?"

"What?" Irene blurts.

"I don't know. I'm sorry. I just thought you might be."

"No, but if you're saying you'd like to talk with someone on this boat who is, I can set that up," Irene says. "Discretely and privately." She continues to sketch, wondering if she should have revealed that. Bob seems like the real thing, a nice guy, and she's usually a good judge of character. But she's taking a risk.

"So there really is a cop on this boat?" he asks.

Irene hesitates, not sure if she should just come out and say it. "Yes."

Bob leans closer. "Ask me tomorrow," he whispers. "I like what you say about your husband – you're helping me think through some things. I'll know a lot more about my situation tomorrow. " He nods toward the door and Irene turns to see Dorothy DeGroot and, she assumes, her husband Dutch, an odd little man in his 60s with balding hair, probably a foot shorter than his striking wife.

Dorothy walks right up to their table. "I see the sketcher found a willing subject," she declares.

"Yes," Irene replies, "a most cooperative and pleasant young man."

She turns her sketch pad so Dorothy can view it.

"That's darn good. Remember, you owe me."

"I'm afraid I must excuse myself," Irene replies, sliding a $5 bill under the corner of her glass, "but it's nice to run into you again. Is this your husband?"

"Yes," Dorothy says, "Irene Johnson this is my husband, Mr. Dutch DeGroot." Dutch extends a limp hand and winces when Irene gives it a good squeeze.

"Sorry, my fault," Irene says. "I keep doing that."

"We actually can't stay, either," Dutch says, turning to Bob. "Mr. Harlowe would you join us back at the cabin? We can talk more easily there."

Irene precedes them out of the bar and turns toward the forward observation lounge. Pausing in the hallway to rummage in her bag for a pen, she watches the DeGroots and Bob Harlowe exit the lounge toward the stateroom area, followed a moment later by the two bikers and the raincoat man. Nobody is smiling.

*

On the bridge, it's the beginning of a long night for the helmsman and mate. The mate switches the interior lights to red for maximum night vision, but the world outside the ship is a featureless void. Clouds block the moon. Squalls lash the ship one after another, the drops rattling the windows.

They have only their instruments to track their position, which is clear enough thanks to GPS and their electronic chart. They are well away from rocky headlands and outcroppings. The ship's course is maintained by the autopilot, but on a night like this with heavy swells and rain, the mate overrides it, deviating a few degrees to smooth the ride for passengers. Winds push the vessel off course, and he gives the helm several corrections to compensate for it.

At this hour, in this weather, passengers no doubt are hunkered down for the evening.

The mate's principal worry is avoiding other vessels that might be nearby. This is the constant concern of larger ships like the Alaska ferry that share these confined waters with all manner of smaller commercial and recreational vessels.

The mate is aware of a northbound tug and barge several miles ahead, and two fishing boats coming toward them. With known vessels he can predict their likely future course based on established traffic lanes, and their stated destination and adjust his own course to maintain a safe separation, which is especially important on a night with compromised visibility.

But he can't identify all smaller vessels, nor see their lights. As rain hammers the windows, he turns to the radar, which is a mess of clutter. He makes several adjustments to sharpen the resolution and reduce false signals, but on a night like this it is little help.

The night requires his full concentration and a bit of good luck.

Chapter 9
Homer

Homer is a welcome sight to Paul after miles of flying over tundra with two taciturn passengers. The long spit is dramatic and brings back memories of a fun boat ride across Kachemak Bay some years earlier with a girlfriend to the isolated artists' colony of Halibut Cove.

The spit is also a reminder of how fast and powerfully nature can change things in Alaska. Everything is bigger here. He flies past active volcanoes all the time, and sometimes *around* them when they spew ash into the sky. When Mt. Katmai explodes in 1912 it is the largest measured volcanic eruption of the 20th Century.

And that's not to mention earthquakes. Parts of Homer Spit sink eight feet during the Good Friday Earthquake of 1964, submerging them in the bay where they remain to this day.

It is the largest recorded earthquake in North American history, at magnitude 9.2. Underwater landslides and massive tsunamis kill 139 people. Damage in Alaska's principal city of Anchorage is extensive. If one thinks too much about such things, how would they function?

After his dicey landing at Platinum this morning, Paul puts the Cessna down smoothly on the deluxe, 6,700-foot, asphalt runway at Homer. He taxies to Pathfinder Aviation, cuts power and lifts off his headset. Then he pops a window for some marine air.

"Good place for a pit stop and to stretch your legs, and maybe get a bite to eat," Paul suggests. "We'll be at least an hour, probably more, while I fuel up and call my wife. I promised her I would do that when I got back to the known world."

What Paul doesn't say is that he is not married.

While his passengers head toward a coffee kiosk in the terminal building, Paul gets out his cell phone and dials.

Chapter 10
Ketchikan

Brad is up early and on deck in his hoodie as the *Matanuska* enters Tongass Narrows approaching Ketchikan. This is exciting – softly forested Gravina Island on the left and the downtown buildings and houses of Ketchikan on the right. A floatplane rumbles low over the ship, following the channel south. An Alaska Airlines 737 sits poised for takeoff on the runway at the airport, across the channel from the mainland.

Alaskans call Ketchikan Alaska's First City, the first town of any size visitors see as they reach the 49th state. It has rained overnight but is sunny this morning, a gift not taken lightly in a place that gets 141 inches of rain a year. Banks of fog and mist add mystery to the landscape.

As they pass the downtown shipyard of Vigor Industries, Brad admires the youngest vessel of the ferry fleet, the *MV Kennicott*, sitting high in drydock for maintenance. Like all the other Alaska Ferries, it is named for a glacier.

Brad has read that the *Kennicott* is a product of the *Exxon Valdez* oil spill. After that 1989 environmental disaster, the state felt the need for an ocean-certified vessel that could serve not only as a ferry but also to fill a secondary role as a command and logistics center in a future disaster. The *Kennicott* joined the fleet nine years later. It includes a helicopter landing pad, additional communications gear and decontamination showers, among its specialized equipment.

In a few weeks cruise ships will take over this waterfront – three and four at a time. The tourists come for the tram up the mountainside and for Creek Street, the historic red light district that now houses trendy shops and restaurants. The *Matanuska* continues north about two miles past the city center to the ferry terminal on Tongass Avenue.

Irene, meanwhile, is checking the lounge and public areas in search of the pilot, Bob Harlowe. Brad and Shane will go ashore separately, in the best disguises they can muster, and trail the DeGroots at a distance. Irene will join them later and, if the DeGroots don't have their minds set on breakfast at The Landing Restaurant, maybe the three of them will share a full-menu breakfast before re-boarding.

Brad counts about a dozen vehicles rolling off the boat and 20 more waiting to load, a hodgepodge of transportation, much of it likely bound for the commercial hub of Juneau, he figures. His eye falls on two vehicles that stand out, an old motor home and a mud-caked Toyota Tundra with a cargo net stretched across a stack of crates. He wonders what might be in those crates. Everything looks suspicious to him now.

Brad's dreams of a Ketchikan breakfast fall apart when the DeGroots, the two bikers and raincoat man head for the restaurant together. Before they even reach the door, a burly guy in a Carhartt rain bib gets out of a white van and shakes hands with Dutch. He must have come straight from a fishing boat.

With the DeGroots and their party at breakfast across the street, Brad heads back to the ship's cafeteria to enjoy a cup of coffee in peace. Shane has the same idea and stakes out a corner table from which he can see everyone entering and leaving. Brad fills his cup, crosses the room and sits down.

"I'll bet you're sorry you ever ran into me," Shane declares.

"Why do you say that?"

"This is supposed to be a vacation for you and Irene. Instead you're playing cat-and-mouse games, afraid to be seen together, afraid even to show your face in the public areas of the boat."

"That's the unpredictability of life," Brad says. "When we signed up for this trip I promised Irene an adventure. She believes me now. We'll talk about this trip for the rest of our lives."

"But it's really not fair to Irene."

"Seriously? I haven't seen her this animated in years. All of a sudden we're a team again and it feels good."

Shane laughs and shakes his head. "Helluva way to make a team." He cups both hands around his coffee and stares at it, as seconds pass.

"Do you think much about Bella and Stu?" he asks.

"All the time," Brad says. "I'd like to see the DeGroots answer for what they did to Bella. And I still wonder if Stu really had to fly his airplane into a lake. He had some pain going back to his childhood that never got resolved. By the time we got to the bottom of Bella's disappearance, I don't think Stu had much will to go on. He could have fought his cancer but he didn't even try."

"We came close to putting the DeGroots behind bars."

"We'll get there," Brad says. "I'm not done and I know you're not, or you wouldn't be here. That story I wrote for the *Washington Post* hurt them badly. The next one will hurt more, depending on how things play out this week. That'll be my little contribution to this effort."

"Revenge for Bella?"

"Justice. She always tackled the hard stories and wrote the truth. That was also the last thing my brother asked of me before his suicide – 'Tell the truth.'"

"So this is quite personal and painful for you."

"Nobody lives this long without their share of pain. I blame myself for plenty of mistakes, including missing the cries for help from both Bella and my brother."

He goes on, "Pain is the part of getting older I hate the most. But age is also liberating because you don't have so much to fear anymore. You've had a good life. You know how the story's going to end – you just don't know exactly when. You have to decide how to get there with some dignity. Bella fought cancer. She wasn't afraid. She sure as hell wasn't afraid of a couple of two-bit hustlers."

Chapter 11
Wrangell

"Could you at least check his cabin?" Shane asks the purser. The *Matanuska* is under way again, en route to a 30-minute stop at Wrangell before it enters the most scenic stretch of the Inside Passage – the torturous, shallow Wrangell Narrows, where they'll be within shouting distance of homes and cabins.

Shane, Brad and Irene huddle with the purser in his private quarters behind the purser's desk, out of sight from passers-by.

"We don't enter someone's cabin unless there's a compelling reason," the purser explains.

"Passenger safety? Criminal activity?" Brad asks.

"Those would be good reasons if you can support them."

"I talked with Bob Harlowe twice on the way up from Bellingham," Irene says. "He was anxious last night in the bar, worried about an imminent meeting with the DeGroots. We cut our visit short, but before I left he expressed interest in talking with a police officer today. I said I could arrange that."

"Ok."

"This morning I searched this whole boat on the way into Ketchikan. He was nowhere. Brad saw the DeGroots and some others head for

The Landing Restaurant without Harlowe, who was a pilot for DeGroot."

"He's booked through to Juneau," the purser notes. "It's easier than you might think to drop out of sight for a while on the boat. Stowaways do it all the time. Maybe this Bob Harlowe snuck down to the vehicle deck."

"Well there's more," Irene adds. "A California couple, the Evans, said they overheard a commotion last night outside their cabin. They were in their bunks in the stern-facing stateroom but keep the heavy window curtains closed for privacy."

"And they heard . . . ?"

"Raised voices. Some scuffling. Someone said, 'This is your stop, buddy,' and they thought someone else said, 'For the love of god,' and then some laughter. Somebody said, 'That wasn't pretty.'"

"But they didn't get up to look?"

"Oh you know, sometimes it's smarter to mind your own business. They weren't sure if it was horseplay or just what. They were in bed and don't move very fast. By the time Jack got to the window, no one was there. The night was windy and wet, and he couldn't see well. He didn't think much more of it till I asked this morning if they had seen the pilot."

"Ok," he says, reaching for his microphone. "We'll start with something easy." He clicks the microphone switch on his desk. "Passenger Harlowe, Mr. Robert Harlowe, please report to the purser's desk."

"We'll give him a few minutes," the purser says. "If he doesn't show, I'll fill in the captain and we'll look below decks to rule that out. Then we'll see if we should open his cabin."

"Meanwhile," he continues, "we're just coming up on a quick stop in Wrangell – about 30 minutes. One vehicle is getting off and I think three or four are loading."

"Not much time to go ashore," Brad notes.

"It's a shame because there's so much history here. Sheldon Jackson, the famed Presbyterian missionary, really came to the rescue of Wrangell natives in 1877 after Russia sold Alaska to the United States. Their condition was appalling with all the alcohol, disease and exploitation by Russians and Americans. Jackson worked closely with Captain Healy of the US Revenue Cutter *Bear*, who was pretty much the only law enforcement officer at the time."

"I've heard both their names but don't know much about them," Brad said.

"Like many prominent figures in history, their impact had its controversial side," the purser says. "Jackson did a tremendous amount of good, but he was totally committed to Americanizing the natives and stamping out their language, spiritual practices and culture."

"I'm going to need a book on that," Brad said.

"There are plenty of good ones. But if you'd like a smile during our quick stop in Wrangell, run uptown a couple blocks and buy a garnet from the kids at the card table," the pursuer says. "They're cute as hell."

"Wait a minute, what are kids doing with garnets?"

"There's an old garnet ledge a few miles north of Wrangell where local kids chisel garnets out of the rock. Call it a quirk of the local geology. If you had more time there's also a native cultural site a lot closer that you could check out, Petroglyph Beach, but we won't be stopping long enough."

"Tell me about the kids," Brad says.

"They sell the garnets to tourists and make pretty good money.

There's some negotiation and competition among the different kids to get a sale. The whole thing was the idea of a former mayor of Wrangell who bought the land for the Boy Scouts and the children of the town."

"Seriously? And it's worth their while?"

"The more industrious kids make $1,000 or so every summer. But if they give you some line about saving for college, don't take it too seriously. Most of the garnet money ends up as new bicycles."

"Ha – that's funny. Still, it's remarkable that someone had the vision to set this up."

"Yeah, rather brilliant. Tourists get to take home a little piece of Alaska and a story about meeting the Wrangell kids. It's especially good for the younger kids. Those are the ones the tourists gravitate toward. As kids get older, they get outsold and lose interest, so they move on to something else because they can't make as much as their little brother or sister."

"I've got to tell my wife," Brad says, excusing himself and heading back to the cabin.

Moments later he knocks lightly and Irene opens the door.

"Honey," he announces. "I have a little 30-minute adventure for us in Wrangell. We'll let Shane handle the DeGroots. You and I are going to see some kids about some rocks."

Chapter 12
Petersburg

The Matanuska inches ahead between flashing navigation buoys in Wrangell Narrows, changing course at each marker to stay within the twisting channel. Evening is falling and a campfire burns brightly on shore a hundred yards away. Sweet smoke from the fire drifts over the ship and takes Brad back to times he and Irene spent in the mountains of Idaho with their friends of a lifetime, Stu and Amy, both now gone. It's a bittersweet memory.

Brad imagines a family around that campfire, roasting weenies and marshmallows, or maybe good friends talking about their day. Smoke drifts toward the ferry from woodstoves in cozy cabins so close he could shout to the owners. A dog barks. A couple standing on their deck wave to the ship and Brad waves back.

But the acrid smell of the cabin steward's cigarette also reaches Brad's nose. The steward silently appears by the rail and gazes at the cabins as he takes a draw of his cigarette.

"How far to Petersburg?" Brad asks.

"About an hour. The narrows are about 22 miles long. It'll be pretty dark by the time we tie up. There are 60 course changes in this stretch and about 65 lighted markers."

"Phenomenal," he says.

"In some spots we have only a few feet of clearance between the ship's screws and the bottom. The ferries are the largest ships that navigate the narrows. Mostly it's tugs, fishing boats and barges. Cruise ships use the open sea."

Brad is no longer thinking about the DeGroots as he begins a circuit of the outer deck. He can't take his eyes off the scenery and the channel they are threading. The whole effect of this stretch is almost spiritual. At these speeds the engines are hardly noticeable. Ducking inside at the bow, Brad finds conversation has fallen silent in the forward observation lounge. He lingers a while, studying the group, but no one arouses suspicion. They seem absorbed with the view.

He makes his way back to the cabin. Shane and Irene already are there, waiting.

"I was just telling Irene that the purser and I came up with nothing," Shane announces. "I went with him when he checked. The room is empty and there is no sign our friend Harlowe has been there for hours."

"Does anything look disturbed?" Brad asks.

"Not really. His suitcase is on the bunk, along with a jacket. A couple of books are sitting out. When someone takes a shower there's usually water on the shower floor and fog on the mirror for a while afterwards, but there is nothing like that. No water drops on the sink. No smell of soap or shampoo."

"So no evidence he used the room this morning."

"None at all."

"So now what?"

"So now the purser is getting concerned," Shane says. "The crew is going to check IDs of everyone debarking in Juneau, which is Harlowe's destination."

"What about Petersburg?" Brad asks. "That's coming up in a couple of hours."

"They'll check carefully in Petersburg, too," Shane answers, "but it's a very small stop compared to Juneau. It'll be nighttime and not very long, and it's not likely many will bother to step off the boat there. A few kayakers, I'd guess."

"Meanwhile," Brad says, "we have potential murderers aboard."

"The captain is arranging for an Alaska State Trooper to meet us in Juneau for the ride up to Skagway and back," Shane replies.

"Won't the trooper and all these ID checks be red flags for the DeGroots?"

"Maybe, but if it makes them stew a bit, so be it. The crew will tell departing passengers we have a stowaway situation. I believe the officer coming aboard will be in plain clothes."

"Meanwhile," Irene interrupts, "if Bob Harlowe went overboard, shouldn't someone be looking?"

"The captain has already asked the Canadian and US coast guards to check the open waters of Dixon Entrance," Shane says. "Based on what time the Evans' said they heard the disturbance, that's where the ship was. Chances of surviving in those waters are close to zero, but they'll take a closer look just in case. They both patrol that area."

"Darn it anyway," Irene says. "He was a good guy and I think he was ready to tell us what he knew."

"If we could have talked with him he would have made our job on this trip a whole lot easier," Shane says, rubbing his forehead and eyes.

"I think the day is catching up with me," he announces. "I'm going to head back to my cabin and get a little rest before we pull into Juneau." He gets up and opens the door. "Things are about to shift into high gear."

Brad waits till the door clicks shut, then pulls aside the window curtain and looks out at the lights of Petersburg. The boat is nearly dead in the water now. Another big, brightly lit ferry, the *MV Malaspina*, is pulling away from the pier where he assumes the *Matanuska* will tie up.

"You know," Irene says, "I'm not quite sleepy yet. I'm going to step outside for some air and watch the loading and unloading activity, and see who else is out. I'll be back in a little bit."

"Stay safe," Brad says. "I think I'll read for a few minutes and then turn in."

Irene makes her way to the shore-side rail. Two cars with kayak racks drive off the ferry, along with half-a-dozen bicyclists with packs. One car waits to board for the trip north. This will be a very brief stop. She watches the deck crew direct the waiting car aboard and close up the ship. Crew members release hawsers to a terminal attendant in a fluorescent vest, who reels them ashore. The ship's engines rumble and a gap opens between the hull and the pier. They are under way.

FINAL PASSAGE

Petersburg is a storybook scene on this quiet night. Irene is glad she made the effort to stay up. The lights of the town and its many boats must hold a thousand secrets of ordinary people and their Alaska-size dreams on the edge of the civilized world.

Moonlight bathes the snowfields of nearby peaks. This is the prettiest place she's seen on this trip, a pocket of humanity in the heart of wilderness, surrounded by water, mountains, glaciers and forest. She has this moment to herself, the other passengers having retired to their cabins for the evening. She lingers a while, then starts a leisurely circuit around the deck, taking in the view and the aromas of creosoted pilings, fish canneries, fir trees . . .

*

The impact from behind knocks the wind from Irene's lungs and sends her reeling forward, fighting for balance. She grabs wildly for the rail with her right arm and barely catches it, staying half on her feet, unable to breathe. Her heart pounds and her legs fold. She wraps her body over the rail and gasps in shock, staring down at white bubbles where the hull slices through the blackness. Half a minute passes with no air. She's in full panic.

Then, ever so slowly, her diaphragm responds and her lungs draw air. She straightens up and wonders what happened. She is alone on the deck – no passengers, no crew. The ship already is in open water, accelerating toward Juneau.

Chapter 13
Over the Coast

Paul Fisher gives the heavily loaded Cessna a long takeoff roll down the paved runway at Homer. In addition to two passengers and a surprisingly large load of oversized duffel bags, the plane now carries full tanks of fuel for the long flight east. His plan is to follow the coast over Pedersen Glacier and Lagoon to Seward, then on to Valdez, Yakutat and Glacier Bay, then cut across to Haines. It's not the most direct route but is all in U.S. airspace and takes him over several small airstrips where he can set the plane down if weather closes in.

"That's Yakutat off our left wing," Paul announces over his shoulder to the men in back. The plane bounces and dips in a patch of turbulence.

"Just keep this thing in the air," comes the reply.

Notwithstanding the bouncy ride, his passengers seem more relaxed now on this last leg of their long flight from the Bering Coast, laughing and pointing out landmarks when the plane punches into openings in the cloud cover. They settle into small talk and Paul concentrates on his flying, while keeping one ear open for conversation from the back. He's pretty sure his phone call from Homer will catch up with these guys at some point, though he may not be there when it does. That's just as well anyway, because the less they connect him to what comes later, the better.

Paul doesn't know what's in those big duffel bags but he can guess, and his passengers are very touchy about any discussion or handling of them.

"Jesus, that's rough terrain," one of the hunters says to his companion as the plane banks over Glacier Bay.

"Well, the tourists pay good money to see it," his friend laughs.

"Yes, and we'll have some good money of our own if we can get to Haines in one piece. What's the guy's name again?"

"Hank."

"Hank?"

"Dutch said that's all we need to know."

Chapter 14
Juneau

"How is it out there?" Brad asks as Irene opens the door to their cabin.

"A little rough."

"Yeah?"

"I've been made," Irene says. "Somebody flattened me against the rail and knocked the wind out of me."

"My god, honey! Seriously? Are you ok?" Brad asks, throwing back the covers and getting up to hug Irene. "Where were you hit? Is anything broken?"

"No but I'm going to be sore in the morning," going on to describe the impact that sent her flying. "I'm lucky I managed to stay on my feet, but I didn't think I'd ever breathe again."

"Did you see who it was?"

"I didn't see anything. I was busy trying to breathe."

Irene says she thinks someone hit her on a dead run with a sharp blow of both hands to her mid-back.

"You could have gone overboard."

"I don't think that was the intention. I think they were letting me know what they could do."

"Stay here while I go get Shane," Brad declares, pulling on his jeans.

"Watch your back," Irene warns as he opens the door.

*

Ten minutes later, the mood is grim in Brad and Irene's cabin. "I shouldn't have put you in this position," Shane says, looking straight at Irene on the opposite bunk and shaking his head. "These people already took one life on Whidbey Island and probably are responsible for another on this boat, Bob Harlowe. I was wrong to involve you."

"I'm an adult," Irene says. "I make my own decisions with my eyes wide open."

"Well now we need to rethink everything because the stakes are going up. Clearly you got too close to their pilot friend. Whether they know about Brad and me it's hard to say, but they're watching you."

Irene shrugs. "No more late-night walks alone. I'll stick to crowds. Bob, the pilot, came right out and asked if I was police. I took it as a compliment."

Brad interjects, "Maybe we aren't in such a bad position. They've tipped their hand that they have a lot at stake here. In a few hours a plain-clothed state trooper comes aboard. That's a little more muscle for us and another set of eyes."

"Yeah, and in Juneau half the vehicles on this boat will unload, and that many more will come aboard. What in the heck are we looking for?" Shane asks, slapping his fist into the open fingers of his other hand.

"Drugs?" Irene asks.

"Maybe," Shane says. "It's possible. But my gut tells me it's something else."

"Maybe we need a drug-sniffing dog."

"That's not a bad idea," Shane says. "Run him up and down the vehicle deck. Trouble is, he'd probably find so many cars with drugs we wouldn't be any closer than we are now to what the DeGroots are actually doing."

Brad looks up. "We know whatever it is, it involves air service to remote places because that's exactly the business the DeGroots are in. A bush airline in Alaska can make good money, but I'll bet there's even better money in transporting shady people and cargo with no questions asked."

Shane gets up and turns toward the door. "Let's try again to get some sleep. In the morning we'll see if the troopers can fit any more pieces into this puzzle."

*

Brad is up at 5 a.m, getting dressed while Irene gets one more hour of rest after last night's violent incident. In the 24-hour routine of the ferry it is easy to lose track of the days. Brad reminds himself this is Monday, the start of a new work week for most people. He heads outside for a look at downtown Juneau as the boat passes by. This is both the state capital and largest city served by the system, but the terminal is not downtown; it is 11 miles northwest at Auke Bay.

In the brisk air of an April morning, Brad appreciates the warmth of his hoodie. He strolls the deck, where passengers are pulling out cell phones and punching numbers. For most of this trip the boat is beyond the range of cell towers and Internet service, but Juneau is part of the world. The boat approaches the pier broadside and is secured within minutes. Waiting for them is a collection of buses and taxis. Many vehicles are lined up in the holding area to make the short hop by ferry to Haines and Skagway, where they can connect by highway to points throughout interior Alaska and Canada.

Passengers are walking ashore now, and in the crowd Brad observes Dorothy and Dutch walk past the terminal to a black SUV, open the back doors and get inside. The vehicle turns right on Egan Drive and heads toward the city. Turning to go back to Shane's cabin, Brad wonders if staying behind to meet with the trooper is a missed opportunity for him and Shane.

Brad, Shane and Irene are discussing this when a knock comes on the cabin door. It's the purser with a short, stocky man in a buffalo plaid jacket. "This gentleman would like to talk with you folks," the purser explains. The man's complexion is ruddy and Brad wonders if this is another of the DeGroots' people.

"Robert Yuka," the man announces, reaching out with his right hand to Shane, who looks confused.

"Alaska State Troopers," Robert continues. He turns and shakes Brad's hand, then Irene's.

"Please have a seat," Shane says, gesturing to an empty bunk. "Are we ever glad to see you."

Brad is still mulling the name. "Yuka," he repeats. "Is that Slavic?"

"Inuit," the trooper declares with a big grin. "Honest to goodness Alaskan."

"Then you're precisely the man we need," Shane says. He fills Robert in on the tip that led him to shadow the DeGroots on this trip, and the subsequent incidents involving the pilot who disappeared and now the assault on Irene.

"Wait a minute – Haraldsen?" Yuka asks. "The guy on the radio?"

"NPR," Brad says. "All Things Considered."

"I thought that name rang a bell."

"You have NPR here?" Brad asks.

"This isn't the end of the earth," Robert says. "We have NPR all over Alaska, especially in Juneau, the state capital. But listen, I've got some news. We found your missing pilot on a beach on Prince of Wales Island by Dixon Entrance. A Coast Guard Jayhawk from Air Station Sitka spotted the body and lowered a rescue swimmer to recover it."

"So we know he didn't survive. Did the Coast Guard get any ID off him?" Shane asks.

"No, but we're pretty sure it's Harlowe, based on the sketch Mrs. Haraldsen provided," Robert says, nodding Irene's way. "He wasn't in the water that long. The captain faxed your sketch to the Coast Guard. Also, we're running down a tip on two hunters a bush pilot delivered to Haines from the Bering Sea coast with a big load of bags for the ferry. Fish and Wildlife Service has sent an enforcement officer to Platinum to see if he can track down what they were doing out there."

"So," Brad says, "we need to pay close attention to the people who board at Haines and who they talk to."

"That's how it looks to me," Robert says.

∗

In the forward observation lounge, Irene watches passengers return to the ship as time approaches for departure to Haines. A Juneau taxi pulls to a stop as close to the boat as it can get. The tip of a cane emerges from the back seat and plants itself on the asphalt, followed by the arm of the Californian, Jack Evans. He gets to his feet, turns and offers an arm to his neatly coiffed wife, Alta, who gets out behind him. After counting out paper money to the cabbie and showing ID to the crew, they make their way onto the car deck.

There's no sign yet of the DeGroots and their party in the black SUV. Brad, Shane and Robert are back in the room, going over their plan. Robert wants to know why an Idaho couple and a Bellingham police officer are so involved in an Alaska investigation. Shane explains their personal history with the suspects and Brad's long relationship with the woman the DeGroots likely murdered on Whidbey Island.

"This probably isn't like any arrangement you've run into before," Shane tells Robert, "but I've already seen there are some benefits to working with Brad, having a nationally-known journalist on our team. And Irene already has learned more under cover than I ever could have on my own."

In the lounge, Irene finds a spot by the window and sits down stiffly. Her back hurts from last night. She takes out her sketch pad, but before she can start she feels a hand lightly touch her shoulder. She turns to find the Evans standing behind her.

"Mind if we join you?" Jack asks.

"Not at all," Irene responds. "I saw you get out of the taxi a few minutes ago. Did you go into town?"

"We sure did – quite an adventure," Alta replies. "We took the Mount Roberts tram up the hillside overlooking Juneau and the channel. My what a view! You look toward Douglas Island, across the bridge."

"I missed it all," Irene says with a frown. "Brad owes me a re-do."

They laugh.

"I wish we had more time, too," Jack adds. "We toured the raptor center and had lunch at the native corporation's restaurant – very nice."

He laughed. "We were right at the next table from that tall blonde you were talking to the other day, and her funny little husband."

He has Irene's full attention now.

"You never know who you're traveling with on this ferry," Jack adds.

"Why do you say that?"

"I hate to admit we caught a bit of their conversation," Jack says.

"They were talking about walruses, of all things."

"You mean like they hope to see a walrus on this trip?"

"No, like they are in the walrus business – buying and selling. I couldn't make any sense of it. Is that even legal?"

"I have a feeling it isn't," Irene replies. "Hey if you'd be willing to do me a favor, just keep your eyes and ears open. I'm interested to know whatever else you see and hear of their activities."

Jack nods silently.

"It's better if I don't say more, just that they are the subjects of some ongoing surveillance."

"That's all we need to know," Jack agrees. "We're pretty good at keeping our eyes open and our mouths shut."

The ship's public address system interrupts them.

Your attention please; this is the purser speaking. We are about to get under way for Haines, arriving there in 4-1/2 hours. In a few minutes we will pass Vanderbilt Reef, which is actually the peak of an underwater mountain. Our plan is to go around the reef. Nervous laughter breaks out in the lounge.

Some of you may know that in 1918 another ship, the Princess Sophia, ran straight into it in a snowstorm, with the loss of all aboard. It's the greatest marine disaster in Alaska history. We do not have a naturalist aboard today but are fortunate that our chief steward, John Hastings, is also an historian. For those interested, he will be available in the forward observation lounge in about 30 minutes to share the Sophia's story.

"Now that's something I don't want to miss," Jack says. "How about you, Alta?"

"Not the most pleasant of subjects but I'm curious."

"You know, Irene, even today things still go wrong. In 2006, the

FINAL PASSAGE

British Columbia ferry, *Queen of the North,* missed a nighttime course change as it came out of Grenville Channel, struck a ledge and sank. People are still arguing about how it happened. The captain and crew thought they had everyone off, but later determined two passengers went down with the ship.

"In fact," Jack adds, "if you look at Gill Island when we pass by it you'll see two white crosses put their as a memorial."

"My god," Irene says. "There is more to this Alaska travel than I imagined."

Chapter 15
Haines

Irene settles into a comfy chair in the lounge and gets out her sketch pad to await the steward's presentation. She leans back and winces at how sore she feels after the incident on the deck. Why is she surprised?

She is just contemplating her choice of subjects when Dorothy DeGroot appears. "Irene!" she declares with a smile. "I think this is my lucky day. Do you have time for that sketch we discussed?"

"I sure do," Irene replies. "Just killing time till the steward gives his talk."

"What should I do?" Dorothy asks. "How do you want me to pose?"

"Oh don't pose at all, please. I do my best work when the subject doesn't even know I'm around."

"Well that's going to be hard to fake," Dorothy laughs. "I'm acutely aware of you."

Irene wonders if there's a sinister message in those words.

"Just look out the window. Is that Mendenhall Glacier?"

"My gosh, I do believe it is," Dorothy declares. "It's a little north of Juneau. There's just a brief, peek-a-boo view from the ferry."
"Look at the glacier." Irene sketches fast. "I'm getting a nice profile."

"Speaking of profiles . . ." Dorothy says, "I see you all over the ship, talking to people, but never this mysterious husband of yours. You did say you're traveling with your husband, didn't you?"

Irene regrets she ever shared that detail.

"Oh yes, but he's in his own separate, manly world. I'm the social one."

"I would think he'd enjoy a talk about a maritime disaster. Will he be joining you?"

"I don't know," Irene says. "My sketching bores him. He's probably talked his way into a private tour of the bridge or engine room."

"Well I am determined to meet him," Dorothy says. "By the way you're moving a little stiffly today. Is your back bothering you?"

"Oh I guess I slept wrong," Irene says. "Nothing that Ibuprofen won't fix."

The steward, John Hastings, arrives and all eyes turn to the front of the lounge. Irene continues to sketch as he begins to speak. He recounts the end-of-the-season voyage of the *Sophia*, fully loaded with miners and prospectors going home from Skagway to Puget Sound for the winter. When it hit the reef, things didn't look too bad. No one was killed or injured, and the ship still had power and lights. The ship was in communication by radio with would-be rescuers, so they sat nearly two days on the reef, waiting for safer conditions to transfer passengers to a rescue ship. But a storm in the night shifted the vessel off the reef and it went to the bottom, taking all to their death.

The *Sophia* disaster a century ago and the *Queen of the North* sinking a decade ago are reminders, he says, that navigating these waters is never routine. Trouble can happen even with the most experienced crew and the best technology. Today's navigation systems are vastly better than those of a century ago, but the *Queen of the North* proves that nothing and no one is foolproof.

"That's why it's so important to pay attention during the safety briefings we give," he says. "We train extensively for worst case scenarios, but when something goes wrong, no one can guarantee the rescue plan will go right. We have to have backup plans for the backup plans, for those times when Plans A and B are not possible."

He has the group's full attention now.

Irene leans toward Dorothy's ear. "Wow," she says. "This is an earful."

"It just goes to show," Dorothy remarks, "you can find yourself in that icy water in a heartbeat, with nobody there to save you."

Irene shivers. That is unmistakable.

"I don't doubt there's some truth to that," Irene replies, tearing the sketch from her book and handing it to Dorothy. "We all have to watch our backs, especially when we think we can cut corners and get away with it."

Dorothy looks at the sketch, smiles and nods. "You've captured me nicely."

"That's my intention," Irene replies with a smile.

The ship is making good time up Lynn Canal, the final 90-mile stretch to Haines and nearby Skagway. The steward explains it's a natural fjord, not a man-made canal. In fact it's the deepest fjord in North America and one of the deepest in the world, at about 2,000 feet.

"Here's a fun fact for you," the steward adds. "The canal was discovered by Joseph Whidbey of the Vancouver Expedition, the same guy for whom Vancouver named Whidbey Island, Washington. His flagship, *HMS Discovery*, was just 99 feet long and the escort vessel, *Chatham*, was even smaller. For comparison, the *Matanuska* is 408 feet."

He adds, "You're looking at various glaciers and snowfields, and those long scars running down the mountains are avalanche chutes." Haines, he explains, is a working town with a highway connection up the Chilkat River drainage to Canada and then to interior Alaska. So quite a few vehicles from the interior make the long drive via Canada's Yukon Territory to Haines to catch the ferry on our southbound run, to continue to Juneau or the lower 48.

"Skagway was the largest city in Alaska in the summer of 1898, with 8,000 – 10,000 residents, almost entirely gold prospectors. Today, honestly, it has become almost a theme park," he says. "It has a winter population of under 1,000. That number doubles in the summertime to serve nearly a million visitors. It's the northern headquarters of the Klondike National Historical Park, the southern headquarters being in Seattle. Right now it's still the off season so you'll find some of the shops and entertainment venues closed, but still plenty to see during our layover there."

The steward points to a cluster of buildings and homes the ship is passing on the left. "That's downtown Haines," he says. "Unfortunately we aren't going there. We'll tie up at the ferry terminal a few miles out of town. It'll be a fairly quick stop, but we'll stop longer when we return later today to pick up the southbound traffic."

The terminal is just coming into view and Irene notices the holding area is quite full. She supposes travelers with vehicles arrive hours early to get space on the boat. At the edge of the lot she notices an old truck with dog compartments. Two men are playing with several huskies.

She knows from following the Iditarod race on the Internet that she's looking at a dog truck and a whole team of Huskies. She wonders who the mushers are. If she can catch up with them, she might recognize their names.

"All right," she says aloud to herself. "Maybe I'll get some dog time yet."

Chapter 16
Skagway

Irene tells Brad and Shane her plan to get some dog time while the boat is at the Haines terminal, then returns to the rail to watch the ship tie up. Robert Yuka goes off to interview the Evans in their stern stateroom for every detail they can remember of the scuffle they heard in Dixon Entrance.

While Irene waits for the ok to go ashore, she watches several large marine mammals swim nearby in a circling pattern, their whiskered faces scanning the view just above the surface. Every so often they arch their backs and dive, coming up a moment later somewhere else with a loud snort and a cloud of mist.

"Those are California sea lions," the cabin steward informs her. "We have quite a run of eulachon around the terminal right now and they're easy pickings for the sea lions."

"What in the world are eulachon?" she asks.

"Basically an oily smelt or candlefish, about six to eight inches long. The natives used to catch them with weirs and nets. They're known by quite a few names. My favorite is Hooligan, spread by someone who didn't hear the name right, I guess."

Irene laughs. "Hooligan. That's what I'm calling them from now on."

"Touché," the steward declares. "That's why we can't stamp it out!"

The captain announces passengers are free to step off the boat for about 45 minutes if they like, and Irene makes her way to the terminal parking lot.

"That's a beautiful dog," she calls out to the two men playing with a white husky by the dog truck. "I miss my boy, Bear, back in Idaho."

"Then you'd better say hello to Willer," the older man suggests. "She's a very social girl, and we like to give these dogs all the experience with people we can. Makes it easier for them in a racing situation where they come into contact with veterinarians and race officials at every check point." Irene kneels down and Willow sniffs and licks her hands and then her face, tail wagging playfully."

"They always know a dog lover," Hank laughs. "Stop her if it's too much."

"No, I want more. I'm deprived. And you're mushers?"

"Yes, Ma'am, Hank Hickok and my ignorant son Trek." Irene is briefly shocked but Trek doesn't hear this because he's plugged into a personal music system.

"When the boat comes back from Skagway in a few hours we'll ride down to Juneau for the tourist season. We spend summers giving dogsled rides to tourists who helicopter up to the glaciers."

"Good lord."

"Well seriously, it keeps the dogs working in the off season so they're in shape for mushing in the winter back home. And if you're trying to support yourself by mushing, you piece together an income any way you can."

Trek is disengaged from this conversation and is leaning with his butt against the truck, texting and also gyrating to something coming from his earbuds. "Forgive my son," Hanks says. "He lives in a different world. Harder to train him than the dogs."

"I thought huskies would be larger," Irene says.

"No, the smaller breeds really are the best for mushing."

"So where's home for you Hank?"

"Two Rivers, outside Fairbanks. We have quite a community of mushers there – best in the nation."

"I thought I picked up a little Texas in your accent."

"Yes, we moved up to Alaska about 10 years ago. But how about you? Where's home for you?"

"Stanley, in the Sawtooth Mountains of Idaho."

"Oh boy, I like the sound of that."

"It's a beautiful place. Winters are hard."

"Can't be hard enough," Hank says.

Back on the *Matanuska,* Dorothy and Dutch watch all this from the rail with hate in their eyes.

"How in the *hell* does she do it?" Dorothy asks. "That woman is everywhere."

A stocky man in a buffalo plaid jacket appears at their side and smiles. "Beautiful day, isn't it?"

*

Irene finishes with the dog and stands up. "Maybe I'll see you again on the boat on the trip down to Juneau," she says.

"Only if you're up in the night," Hank says. "We board about 10 o'clock tonight and get off before dawn. Heckuva schedule but with the ferries it's all about making time."

Irene takes a short walk along the shore for a better look at the sea lions and their Hooligans. She snaps a few pictures – perhaps to use in a sketch later. Then she heads back to the terminal and waits with a few arriving foot passengers till the captain announces departure for Skagway. The agent gives the all-clear and they walk onto the car deck. She understands by water this is a one-hour hop, shortest of the entire trip, though by land Skagway and Haines are 775 miles apart. Thanks to Alaska topography, the highway takes the long way around through Canada.

In Shane's cabin, Robert Yuka has some news for Brad and his detective friend. "We have a federal wildlife officer coming aboard in Skagway."

"So do we have enough on the DeGroots to close the net?" Brad asks. "I'm getting tired of sneaking around. I wouldn't mind playing tourist in Skagway with Irene, since we'll be in port for a few hours."

"We don't know how all the pieces fit yet," Robert says, "but we do have a description of two hunters who flew from Platinum to Haines with a large load of suspicious bags. Fish & Wildlife found about 18 walrus carcasses out on the coast that were missing their tusks and baculums. Several were missing their entire skulls. All that raw ivory is a financial windfall in the hands of the right buyer. Natives can harvest walrus for subsistence but it's illegal for non-natives to hunt, sell or trade the ivory, or transport it out of the United States."

"Weren't those hunters taking a risk of being turned in by the pilot who flew them from the coast?" Shane asks.

"We think they probably intended to fly on DeGroot Air, but there was no pilot available to pick them up, and they needed to catch this ferry. They ended up with an unfamiliar pilot who has a conscience and a bad feeling about them."

"So now we just have to identify them when they board with the contraband and turn it over to the DeGroots, right?" Brad asks.

"Yes and the federal wildlife officer will take the lead on that, with as much help as we can give him."

With the investigation now shifting to the hands of state and federal officers, Brad and Irene excuse themselves and head back to their cabin.

"When we get to Skagway, let's go ashore separately so we don't attract attention and then meet a few blocks uptown. We can at least share an ice cream cone and visit a bookstore, see a bit of what's there," Brad says. "This place is loaded with Gold Rush and railroad history. We should get a taste of it."

The ship proceeds to the very head of Lynn Canal and docks bow-first, facing uptown. Skagway is boxed in by mountains on the left and right, resulting in a long and narrow community. Just a few blocks away, a locomotive of the White Pass and Yukon Railway sits on exhibit for tourists. A rotary snowplow on the front almost dwarfs the rest of the engine.

"The purser tells me there's a bookstore, Skagway News Depot, a few blocks away," Brad says before heading out in his hoodie. "Give me a five minute head start and let's meet there."

He keeps his head down in case anyone's eyes are on him.

In the ship's observation lounge, Dorothy and Dutch study the passengers straggling off.

"That guy," Dorothy says. "In the hoodie. There's something about him."

"Maybe this is his stop," Dutch replies. "His destination."

"Not without luggage or a backpack. He's been invisible since Bellingham. The few times I've seen him, he's been in that hoodie. If he gets back on the boat when we leave, I think we'd better take him seriously."

"The boys can handle any lifting."

"You'd better be right because if things unravel, we've got no place to go on this boat."

"Don't worry, my dear. It's all arm's length. Mr. Nguyen is keeping a safe distance. If anyone's watching, they're looking in the wrong places for the wrong people. We're just, what's the word, facilitators."

"I hope you're right."

"Now we'd better hustle uptown and meet our lunch guest," Dutch suggests. "I want to make sure he's on board with his assignment."

At the Skagway News Depot, Brad's eye lands right away on a book by the nationally-renowned Haines journalist and author, Heather Lende, *If You Lived Here I'd Know Your Name*. She's a master of his kind of journalism, the hometown stories and larger-than-life goodness of everyday people. He makes a mental note to buy the book, but then spots another he also wants about Soapy Smith, the legendary Skagway con artist and hustler who cheated boatloads of gold prospectors of their stake before his death in an 1898 gunfight with the town marshal.

Brad is just getting into Soapy Smith's story when the bell on the shop door dings. He looks up as Irene enters and walks over to him.

"This guy," Brad says, "was something else," holding up the book for Irene to see the front cover. "Prospectors streamed into Skagway at the turn of the century to seek their fortunes, and Soapy Smith made his without ever lifting a shovel – by fleecing them of their stake as they came ashore."

"You seem right up to speed on local history," Irene says.

"It's from all the reading I did before we left home. For three years from 1896 – 1899 about 100,000 prospectors came north for the Klondike Gold Rush. They all had to get over the mountains to the Yukon, and the routes they took started either here or in Dyea, in the next inlet a few miles away. Fortunes were made, but mostly by retail merchants and others who sold goods and services. The Gold Rush was big business in Seattle, the jumping off point."

"Well from what we know so far of the De Groots, this is still a state where con artists and crooks can do well," Irene said, gesturing grandly at the street.

"Oh shit," Brad exclaimed. "Speaking of them . . ."

Across the street, the odd couple – Dorothy and Dutch – walk their way. "You'd better get out the door now," he tells Irene. "Odds are they're coming here. I'm going to ask the clerk if this shop has a back door and slip out that way."

On board the *Matanuska*, Shane takes advantage of the strong cell signal to place a call. It rings several times and his wife Judy picks up.

"How's everything at home?" he asks.

"We're fine. The school wants money for Billy's band uniform."

"Send me the amount. Is he there?"

"Yes and he'd like to talk with you." There's a pause while she hands the phone to Billy.

"Are you in Alaska?" Billy asks.

"Yes I am. Go to Google Earth and find a place called Skagway. That's where I am for a few hours. Then the ship will start back to Bellingham."

"Did you arrest somebody?"

"Not yet but I'm working on it. I'm going to surprise them when they don't expect it." Shane thinks a moment, then adds, "You remember our friend Bella, who lived next door?"

"She liked birds."

"She was a nice lady. And you remember she died and we didn't think it was an accident."

"Yes."

"Well, I think the people who did it are the ones I'm tracking."

"I hope you get them."

"I hope so, too," Shane says. "I'll let you know how it turns out."

*

"Robert and Shane talk in Shane's stateroom. Light tapping at the door interrupts them and Shane gets up to answer. It's an outdoorsy young woman, petite, with a blonde ponytail, in form-fitting jeans and a Cabelas baby blue T-shirt. A moose logo and "It's My Nature" lettering complete the package. Her left arm holds the hanger of a garment bag slung over her shoulder.

"Don't worry; I'm not moving in with you guys," she announces with a grin and a head fake toward the bag. "I just thought I should say hello before I get settled. You're the trooper and the Bellingham detective, I understand."

"Yes," Shane replies, "and you are?"

"Marie Martin, U.S. Fish & Wildlife Service. My uniform's in the bag." She shakes hands with each of the group.

"Go ahead and hang your bag from the upper bunk rail," Shane says, "and have a seat." He gestures to a spot for her on the lower bunk and closes the door.

"Sorry, we're a little crowded here."

The door is barely closed when another knock comes.

"I've got it," Robert says, getting up and opening the door to find

Brad. "Come in, please," Robert says, "and meet our federal wildlife officer." He makes introductions.

"You're back soon," Shane says.

"It got a little hot for us in town," Brad replies. "The DeGroots almost caught us together at the bookstore."

Robert fills in Marie on why he's working with a Bellingham detective and an Idaho journalist, and their history with the DeGroots. He also explains that Brad's wife is their best undercover operative on the boat. He tells Marie that someone in the DeGroot party likely threw a pilot overboard who was on the verge of revealing what he knew. For the Alaska state troopers that makes this is a murder investigation.

"So," Brad cuts in, "how can we help you, Marie? What's the plan from here?"

"Optimally, it's to put eyes on those two hunters who flew to Haines. They should board the ferry tonight in Haines and, we assume, transfer their walrus ivory at some point to the DeGroots. We'd like to catch them all with their hands on the evidence."

Brad senses the potential in these developments for a compelling national story on illegal hunting and ivory trade on the Last Frontier.

"What is it about walruses that makes it worth taking these risks?" he asks.

"Supply and demand," Marie replies. "That and because ivory is such a fine-grained natural substance, with a mellow tone and glowing color. A lot of elephants were destroyed to become piano keys and billiard balls. With the rampant poaching of elephants in Asia and Africa to fill the worldwide demand for ivory, the species is threatened with extinction in the wild, and many countries are cracking down hard on trafficking. That's pushing up demand for Pacific Walrus ivory, even though these animals also are protected."

"I thought there was no way to get ahold of raw ivory," Brad said.

"Alaska natives can hunt walrus for subsistence purposes as long as they don't waste it, and they can sell the tusks to non-natives if they first transform them into art. Fossilized ivory can be bought and sold freely, but non-natives are strictly prohibited from buying or owning raw ivory."

"I can't believe these animals are hunted just to become tourist trinkets and artworks."

"Oh it goes further," Marie says. "There's quite a demand for the skulls and baculums, too."

"Baculums?"

"Penis bones," Marie declares with a grin. "Those are extra special, it seems." She rolls her eyes.

"Who buys all this ivory and animal parts?" Brad asks.

"There's a big demand in Asia. Much of it ends up there, where entire factories of artists transform it into pieces for sale. Prince William went on Chinese TV a few years ago to speak out against the use of ivory, if that gives you some idea."

She continues, "Hunting lodges and private collectors find that a walrus skull with the tusks attached is quite a draw, too. Of course when displayed in a public place it has to be clearly aged and have the right documentation about how it was acquired. Put one of those in the lobby of a hunting lodge and it's the first place people go when they enter the room."

Brad listens and stares at his hands.

"So it's safe to assume the DeGroots are the middlemen on this. If they brokered an illegal walrus hunt on the Bering Sea coast, they must have a buyer."

"Yes, that's someone we'd very much like to identify and apprehend."

Marie sighs and continues. "I don't know if we're winning or losing anymore. The new administration in Washington is tying our hands, cutting budgets, dismantling entire departments and dropping environmental protections." We have one of the president's tweets framed on our wall for inspiration: *'Walruses vs. jobs. That's a no-brainer.'*"

"He's fostering a permissive climate in which people like the DeGroots feel they have a sympathetic administration in the White House and are freer to play fast and loose. It's demoralizing, you can imagine. Suddenly we have the prospect of more oil drilling and pipelines and coal mining hanging over us, eating away at what's left of the wildlife and native lifestyle. There's less vigilance about toxic chemicals and groundwater pollution. The whole fragile system is more vulnerable to short-sighted exploitation."

"I certainly know we're backing away from science and the nation's commitment to fight global warming and ocean acidification," Brad says. "I've read a great deal about that."

"Yes," Marie adds, "and you know the glaciers are melting like crazy all over Alaska. We're losing the permafrost that has kept vast areas stable for thousands of years. That releases methane into the atmosphere. Villages are having to move to higher ground because shorelines are eroding."

"It's a shocking picture," Brad says. "I hadn't realized walruses were part of it, but this explains a lot. If you'll excuse me I'd better go check on my wife. I left her uptown with the DeGroots. Hope she makes it back to the boat without any more incidents."

Chapter 17
Turnaround

"I don't think they saw me," Irene tells Brad back in the room. "They went into the bookstore for a while and I watched from across the street. Dutch kept checking his watch and made a call on his cell phone. A few minutes later they headed for the only café that was open.

"Some guy in those fancy, gold-rimmed aviator glasses joined them. I could see that through the café window but couldn't get anywhere near them to hear what they were discussing. They were pretty engrossed."

"So describe this guy," Brad asks.

"Average height, 30s, nice looking, fit, clean-shaven – not your typical backwoods type."

"Pilot, maybe?"

"He had that bearing – like he's very capable and responsible. But that reminds me, did Bob Harlowe have any relatives or family?"

"A sister," Brad says. "Elizabeth. According to Robert, his parents are deceased."

"So will she identify the body?"

"I think so. She's flying to Sitka."

"From where?"

"Auburn, Washington, near Sea-Tac airport. That's her home."

"So he had no wife or girlfriend?"

"None that the police were able to find. Just the sister."

*

At the ship's rail, Robert and Marie look the part of a typical Alaska couple. They watch vehicles roll onto the boat, noting the ones they'd like to check more closely on the trip south. They already have permission from the captain to access the vehicle deck between ports, when passengers are prohibited from that area. Their best lead remains the tip from the Bering Sea pilot about the two hunters he delivered to Haines with suspicious cargo. So Haines is where the real scrutiny will begin. When passengers purchase their tickets for the ferry they automatically consent to security screening of their vehicles and person, and must comply with state, federal and local laws.

This gives Robert and Marie some leverage to be intrusive if necessary. They have the full cooperation of the captain and crew, but the crew's priority is to maintain the unforgiving schedule. They are already spread thin by their wide-ranging duties and the challenges of equipment that inevitably breaks down in the course of any round-the-clock operation.

Brad joins Robert and Marie at the rail in his hoodie and dark glasses. "I was just back by the cafeteria," he says. "Half-a-dozen crew are carrying sacks of potatoes and other provisions up the stairs from the car deck."

"It's the damn elevator," Robert says. "Ferry personnel fight this all the time. The elevator breaks down and the crew has to make do till they can rendezvous with a technician somewhere for a few hours."

"Wow, as if they weren't under enough pressure."

"They work hard," Robert says. "Budgets get tighter every year and the system operates at a loss, so it's a constant juggle between safety and efficiency. All the crew are generalists and pitch in wherever they're needed at the moment, including officers. It's kinda like the troopers. Many of us are pilots and fly ourselves wherever we need to be."

"So you fly, too, Robert?" Marie asks.

"Yes, ma'am, I do."

"Man of many skills."

"Well, we've done all we can to prepare for what's coming up," Brad says. The ship is just pushing away from the dock. "What a gorgeous day it has been in Skagway – 80 degrees so early in the season."

"That happens more than you'd expect in the springtime," Marie remarks. "Skagway can really surprise you."

"I think we're in for some bigger surprises in Haines," Robert remarks as the ship's engines accelerate. He excuses himself to go back to his cabin and make some calls before he loses a cell signal.

In the narrow, upper reaches of Lynn Canal, walled in by steep mountains on both sides, the horizon is high on the hillside and the sun goes down early. The water is glassy smooth and Brad feels at peace after a busy day. Evening is starting and it's a short hop back to Haines and the holding area full of vehicles.

"Feel like a cup of coffee, Marie?" Brad asks. They head to the cafeteria.

"We haven't had much chance to get acquainted," he says. "I thought we might do that now before things ramp up." They find seats in a quiet corner.

Brad explains how he got involved in the DeGroot investigation, going back to Bella Morelli, his first love after he graduated from the

University of Washington in the 1960s.

"That must have been awkward with your wife," Marie ventures.

"We were at a bad point and it sure didn't help that I took off for Whidbey Island to find out what happened. But after Shane and I took the investigation as far as we could and I wrote the newspaper article, I think Irene and I both were ready to put it behind us and move on."

"She's a real bulldog about the DeGroots," Marie says.

"That's Irene," Brad laughs. "She loves an adventure. But tell me about you. Wildlife enforcement is dangerous work for a young woman, isn't it?"

"You mean how did I feel about getting shot a couple years ago?"

"Seriously? You were shot?"

"Just the leg. Man, I was pissed! You should have seen the other guys. I arrested a couple of poachers in the Brooks Range. I'm fine now – don't limp any more."

"And it's worth it to you?"

"I love this job and really believe in what we do. Growing up here we live with the magnificence of wildlife all around us – bears in the creek, moose in the road, thousands of walruses barking. Nature is all around us, and these animals aren't just dollar signs but part of our psyche."

"I can tell it's way more than a job."

"Everyone in the agency feels exactly the same. We come up against these survivalist types, religious cults, greedy exploiters and god knows what else – people who believe the laws are burdensome and don't apply to them. They hate the feds. But as long as I'm here, they'd better look over their shoulder. If I can find them, I'm going to spoil their day."

"So how did you end up in this job?"

"Oh, it fell into place. Dad was in the Air Force in Fairbanks. He took us hiking, camping and fishing constantly. I went to the University of Alaska and studied biology and conservation management. I knew I wanted an outdoor job."

"No boyfriend?"

"Not for lack of trying. My luck with men isn't good. But I kinda like what I see of that cute Robert Yuka, don't you?"

Brad gulped his coffee and smiled. "Yeah, I like him too. I think he's a straight shooter."

The ferry makes fast progress on this still evening. When the Haines terminal comes into view, Brad thinks the scene isn't much different than when they were here a few hours ago. But it feels like the cat and mouse game with the DeGroots is about to turn serious.

"Time to go to work," he says, and they both get up. "Thanks for the company."

The ship approaches the dock confidently. Side thrusters close the gap. Deck crew throw lines and the terminal agent makes them fast to cleats on the dock. The captain gives the ok for passengers to step ashore but few accept the offer this time. They've just had hours of shore time in Skagway, a big day in the warm sunshine, and there is little more to see here, miles from the town center, as evening arrives.

Brad notices the Raincoat Man is on deck now, a rare show of interest from him. When Dorothy and Dutch appear at the rail some distance away, Brad decides it's time to go back to the cabin and leave the people watching to Robert and Marie.

*

The increasing rumble of the ship's engines is Brad's first clue they're leaving Haines, an hour-and-a-half later. A knock at the door is the second.

It's Robert and Marie. The five of them, including Shane and Irene, are a tight fit in the small cabin.

"Well that was perplexing," Robert says. "We eyeballed every single person and vehicle boarding the boat and watched the stairs as they climbed up from the car deck. It was mostly couples. In a way I'm glad the elevator is out of service. We saw no hunters – no one matching the description of the two men the pilot delivered to Haines."

"So what does this mean?" Brad asks. "The DeGroots aren't just along for the scenery. We're on our way back to Bellingham now."

"It could mean the tip was a false lead," Robert says. "Or the hunters aren't traveling with the bags any more. Or the bags are coming aboard somewhere else. Or they're already aboard, from Skagway."

Marie cuts in. "The DeGroots seemed pretty interested in the loading process at Haines. I don't know if they would have stood at the rail that whole time unless they were watching for someone."

Irene remarks, "We aren't making much progress here. I'm going to take a swing through the lounge. See if anyone's around. I met some mushers when I went ashore earlier and maybe I'll find them up there."

"Watch your back," Shane warns.

"I could use a cup of coffee," Robert says.

"Me, too," Brad replies, "I'm beyond knowing if it's morning or night anymore."

"I'm good," Shane says.

"I'll pass as well," Marie adds. "Coffee at this hour screws me up."

Brad and Robert head for the cafeteria.

"I had a few minutes for a nice talk with Marie today," Brad says.

"She's easy to talk to, don't you think?" Robert replies.

"Yeah but don't go up against her in a gunfight."

"You heard about that?" Robert laughs. "A lotta scumbags hate the feds. It's not right. Nice girl like Marie."

"What about the staties? How is it for you being a trooper?"

"You mean as a native? There's respect for the uniform. People know if they get into trouble, we are there for them. There may be only one trooper and he'll come to their aid. That's how it is with the troopers. The little villages, you know, like Umkumiut where I was born, don't have anyone but a VSO – Village Safety Officer. Something happens, somebody gets drunk and shoots somebody, and one of us flies in to deal with it, pretty much no matter what the weather. Big state. We work alone mostly."

"This must be different for you, working plain clothes."

"Yeah, it feels weird. The uniform gives me a little gravitas I don't have as a native walking around in a wool shirt."

"Funny," Brad says, "I was talking with a woman who noticed you and thought you cut a pretty handsome figure in the buffalo plaid."

"Come on, you're playing with me."

"No, absolutely serious."

"She's on this boat?"

"She is. Alaska-born, nice looking, smart, likes to fish and hunt."

"Married?"

"Single."

"Boyfriend?"

"In between."

"Does she like seal meat?"

"I didn't ask. Is that a deal breaker?"

"Not if those other things are true."

"I think you'd like her. You should have coffee with her."

"And you're sure she likes me?"

"She thinks she does."

"Can you point me in her direction?"

"Yeah, I think I can do that."

*

In the lounge, Irene finds her California friends Jack and Alta sitting with an older woman she has seen several times on the trip north but not yet met. It seems many of the faces in the room are familiar – passengers going back on the same boat that brought them north.

Jack looks up and sees Irene approaching. "Come over and join us, Irene. How is your trip so far?"

"Wonderful," she says. "All of this is new to me."

"This is Frances Pedersen of Seattle," Jack says, in turn introducing Irene to Frances. He describes Irene as a horse rancher from Idaho married to 'that famous journalist with the radio program.'

"Are you traveling alone?" Irene asks.

"No, with two of my brothers – sort of a geriatric family reunion on the boat. Our dad lived in Seward and Skagway as a boy."

"Wow, so you really have a personal connection to Alaska."

"Yes, we walked uptown to the Presbyterian Church, where our grandfather was the minister shortly after the Gold Rush period. They say the church is little changed from a century ago. The pews are actually opera seats. Our dad was a teenager then and sold newspapers on the White Pass and Yukon Railroad."

She continues, "The family was very prominent in the community, which wasn't very large at that time. In fact one of our uncles was the newspaper editor for a while, and three of the boys sold photography from a shop on State Street known as Pedersen Brothers. There's a famous postcard of the train going up the middle of the street with the Pedersen Brothers sandwich board right in front of it."

"Oh boy, what a nostalgia trip for you."

"Yes, Dad told all these Alaska stories growing up, but we could never keep them straight. You know how it is when you're a kid – you don't pay much attention. It helps to lay eyes on the geography. The stories start to make sense."

"I can't believe all these family connections you have," Irene says.

"So is the trip living up to your expectations?"

"Oh yes, and I'd do it again just for the people-watching. There are so many characters on this boat, and now I've just met another," she says with a wink and a smile for Irene. "That's half the fun."

Irene replies, "Two mushers came aboard with their dogs in Haines. I talked with them in the holding area and thought I might catch up with them again here in the observation lounge but no luck."

"They were here a few minutes ago," Frances says. "I saw them talking with some people and then they all left together."

"You don't happen to remember the people they were talking to, do you?" Irene asks.

"Oh that's easy," she says. "It was that short-and-tall couple."

Chapter 18
Juneau Southbound

"I think we've got a break," Irene announces to her colleagues as she opens the door to the stateroom. "Someone told me they saw the DeGroots walk out of the observation lounge with the dog mushers."

Robert replies he will get the mushers' names from the purser and request a background check right away from Anchorage. If they have a history with law enforcement, it could tell them a lot.

"Where the heck were they going just now?" Brad asks.

"Well it can't be the car deck because no one can access it except the crew," Robert replies.

"Oh no!" Shane groans, looking up suddenly. "They don't have someone on the inside, do they, on that deck crew?"

"It's possible," the wildlife officer, Marie, acknowledges. "It would sure help if we knew who we could really trust. Everyone on this ship reports to the next guy up. If the crew is in on it, the question is how far up does it go?"

"Realistically," Robert says, "how many people can the DeGroots have in their pocket? There can't be that many. They're new at this and it takes time to build a network."

Marie cautions against assuming too much or moving too fast against the mushers. "If the mushers brought the ivory on board and have it in their possession, it's doubtful they are the actual buyers – a boy and his dad. They don't fit the profile of anyone I've ever known to engage in the ivory trade, nor do they likely have the right resources to alter it for the consumer market. So far we haven't caught the DeGroots doing anything Irene didn't do – namely, talk to these guys. We need more than that."

"Jeez these people cover their tracks," Shane groans.

Brad interjects. "I hate to bring this up but we started with a description of two hunters who might or might not be up to something. They never boarded at Haines. Now we're looking at mushers who have no known connection to the hunters who never boarded, and who may have nothing to do with anything. They may be a red herring while the real transaction happens somewhere else."

"Right," Robert says, "we're grasping at threads. I think we need to keep our eyes on the DeGroots. They are the key to this jigsaw. If there's a reason to intercept the mushers I can arrange for that in Juneau. But I think the ivory will be where the DeGroots are."

"Well perhaps we should all get a few hours rest between now and

2:30 a.m.," Brad says. "When we get to Juneau we'll need to be on our toes. Juneau is your destination, isn't it, Robert?"

"Originally," Robert says. "That *was* my plan. But I still have an unsolved murder and two smuggling suspects to follow so I'll stay with the boat."

Brad can't help thinking life on ship is increasingly unmoored from everything – night and day, the day of the week, and geographic location, since they're constantly on the move. He wonders how the crew gets used to it – rotating on and off a few at a time at various ports for two-week shifts of 12 hours, sometimes working alongside the same crewmates and sometimes not.

As they approach Juneau's Auke Bay terminal Brad notices dozens of cars and trucks waiting in the darkened holding area, drivers and passengers presumably resting their eyes but getting little sleep. From time to time, loudspeakers blare instructions about lanes and loading priorities to those who wait.

The ferry ties up at 2:30 a.m. and unloading begins. No one leaves the boat at this hour for sightseeing in town. Nothing is open; there's nothing to see.

From his stateroom window, Brad watches a few dark figures straggle off the boat, bent forward against the weight of backpacks on their shoulders. In the shadows it's impossible to recognize specific people. The mushers' truck drives ashore with other vehicles.

Nearly all the departing vehicles turn right toward the downtown area but the mushers turn left, drive a block and then stop to pick up a hitchhiker. The guy peels off his backpack and climbs up into the cab. Brad thinks it's a lonely hour to be out on the street, miles from city center. Maybe Alaskans are used to it, with their 24-hour transportation system.

A knock on the door brings Robert, Marie and Shane.

"The mushers check out," Robert says. "Anchorage has nothing on them but a couple of equipment violations – defective tail light and so on. Hank Hickok is well known in the mushing community. In the summers he gives dogsledding demonstrations in the mountains above Juneau. The cruise passengers eat this stuff up – you know, helicopter rides to the glacier, and a photo op at the controls of a dogsled. It's a good niche for Hickok and I doubt he would do anything to screw it up."

"I was just wondering," Brad says, "what is out to the left of the terminal on the Glacier Highway, if you turn away from the city center."

"Not much," Robert says. "Seafood processing, a few homes and industrial buildings, floatplane docks, campgrounds. My yoga class meets out there. The road ends a few miles from town."

"I noticed the mushers turned that way instead of toward town," Brad points out.

"They may have a place in mind to park their truck for the night and get some rest before morning," Marie says.

"It's going to be cozy in that cab trying to nap with the hitchhiker they picked up," Brad says.

"Is it someone who got off the boat?" Robert asks.

"It looked that way."

"Ok, then we've got a problem."

Robert gets on his cell phone to the Juneau Police, requesting assistance locating a dog truck on the Glacier Highway beyond Auke Bay. He asks them not to approach the occupants but to observe and report to him. Multiple units are responding to an armed domestic violence call in Mendenhall Valley with a potential hostage, and will check on the dog truck as soon as they can free up an officer.

Shane heads to the purser's desk for the names of passengers booked to debark in Juneau this morning. The purser is swamped assigning staterooms and issuing keys to the groggy arrivals.

*

By the first light of the predawn, two men in dark clothing lug oversize duffel bags down a short pier to a float 30 feet from the rocky shore. At this hour hardly any cars pass on the bayside highway. They don't need lights for what they're doing and keep their voices low, since voices carry over water on a still night. "Watch your step," the younger man warns. "This dock picks up condensation overnight and can be slick."

A darkened DeHavilland Beaver is tied fore and aft to cleats on the float. The younger man steps onto the plane's left pontoon and opens the cargo bay.

"So what do we have here?" the pilot asks, looking back at the pile of bags.

"Tourist souvenirs," the older man replies in an Asian accent.

It's not a very helpful answer, the younger man thinks, but this guy clearly wants to minimize discussion.

"Pass me that first bag, will you," he asks. He begins arranging the load as the Asian passes him additional bags. Within minutes the loading is complete and the pilot buttons up the hatch.

He opens the cabin door and gestures to his passenger to climb in. "Make yourself comfortable up front on the right if you like. You'll find a seatbelt and harness. I can help you with the harness if you need a hand. I'm going to untie us and give the plane a little push. Then I'll join you and we'll fire up and taxi a few minutes, and get on our way."

*

Dawn in Juneau in late April comes about 5 a.m., but on a clear morning there's plenty of light long before that. Brad thinks the pink dawn of this particular morning is like something from a watercolor painting. The ship is just pulling away from the dock as the first float plane of the morning rumbles low overhead on its way south – part of the magic and mystery of everyday life on the Last Frontier. It's a DeHavilland Beaver, a classic Alaska workhorse, and even in the soft light he can clearly make out the printing on the fuselage: DeGroot.

He has a bad feeling about this.

Meanwhile, the trip is about to get interesting because they're headed someplace new – the old Russian capital of Sitka. The ferry's southbound run picks up the coastal city as an additional stop.

Brad is just thinking about heading back to the cabin when the chief steward appears at the rail beside him and lights up. He takes a long draw.

"We'll be in Peril Strait soon," the steward announces.

"Something new."

"There are some tight spots," the steward says. "We often see whales in this stretch, or bears on the beach."

"Really?"

"Yeah, if you scan the beach with binoculars you'll usually see them. And a little closer to Sitka we get into sea otter territory. The Russians nearly hunted them to extinction, but they've made a comeback."

"So do we go right into Sitka?"

"No, not directly. You can't get all the way there from here. The terminal is several miles out, but there will be buses to take you to town for a few hours and get you back before departure. It's well worth the trip – full of history and culture, the old Russian Orthodox Church . . . "

It crosses Brad's mind that Sitka airport is headquarters of the Coast Guard station whose aircrew recovered the body of Bob Harlowe back in Dixon Entrance.

"Have you been doing this long – crewing on the ferry?" Brad asks.

"Twenty-seven years, winter and summer," the steward says, then inhales deeply again.

"That's a lot of trips up and back," Brad remarks.

"I've seen it all."

The steward exhales a cloud of blue smoke. "I just love this life and intend to keep doing it till they carry me off the boat feet first, with a sheet over my head." He flicks his cigarette over the side, into the water.

Robert Yuka appears at Brad's side. "Could we have a word back at the cabin?" he asks. Irene, Shane and Marie are waiting there when they arrive.

Juneau Police, he says, located the mushers' truck at a pullout on the Glacier Highway, three miles beyond the Auke Bay terminal. At Robert's suggestion they approached and woke up Hank Hickok and his boy. They were napping in the truck for a few hours before making connections to move all their dogs up to the glacier."

Robert continues, "Juneau PD asked if they'd given a ride to any hitchhikers."

"Yeah, to a creepy guy," Hank's son Trek volunteered. "But he only rode with us for a few miles till he got out."

Hickok seemed a little reluctant to offer details, but finally explained he made arrangements earlier with someone on the ferry to pick up the guy north of the terminal and deliver him to a floatplane dock. He unloaded some bags the Hickoks brought with them from Haines and, last they saw, he and the pilot were loading them onto the plane.

"Jesus," Shane says. "This is shady as hell."

Robert continues. "Juneau PD says Hickok knows the whole transaction wasn't on the up and up. Claims he doesn't know what was in the bags and that it was none of his business, but he knows legitimate people don't do things this way. He wants to cooperate."

"So do we have a description of the passenger who boarded the float plane with the bags?" Marie asks.

"Yeah, Hickok's son says 'creepy.'" Robert adds, "The boy says he had a mustache and a black raincoat, looked kind of Asian or maybe native."

"Oh boy," Irene says. "That sounds like Raincoat Man. Do we know if he left the boat?"

"The purser is working on that," Robert says. "He's booked to Ketchikan but maybe he got off a couple stops early."

"Maybe it was a little warm for him and the DeGroots moved up the plan," Brad says.

"Maybe it was never his intention to go to Ketchikan," Marie adds.

"So now where the hell is that DeGroot airplane?" Shane asks.

"You can bet there's no flight plan," Brad says. "Does DeGroot have an office?"

"All I know of is an answering service in Bellingham," Shane says.

"I'll put out the word to all the float plane outfits in Southeast to let us know immediately if any DeGroot DeHavillands show up somewhere," Robert says. "They can only stay airborne for so long before they have to refuel."

"Do we have a name for Raincoat Man?" Irene asks.

"Nguyen," Robert replies. "Mr. C. Nguyen."

"Probably an alias," Marie says. "He'd be crazy to use his own name."

"So," Brad says, "we know two hunters delivered the bags to Haines, where they handed them off to two mushers, who transported them to Juneau, where Raincoat Man left the boat and took possession of the bags, and flew away this morning on a DeGroot airplane."

"That sums it up in one sentence," Robert says.

"I'm guessing the pilot of that plane was Bob Harlowe's replacement," Brad says, "probably in the same aircraft Harlowe told Irene he was on his way to join in Juneau. And I wouldn't be surprised if the mystery pilot is the same guy Irene saw the DeGroots talk to at the café in Skagway."

"What do we know about the hunters?" Robert asks, looking at Marie.

"They were in and out of Platinum without talking to anyone. No one knows who they are, but we're checking with our people all over the Bering Sea Coast," Marie says.

"Someone has to know something," Robert adds.

Marie continues, "Once they got to Haines and handed off the bags to the mushers, they just disappeared. The way the DeGroots operate, I doubt the hunters know who paid them for the job nor where the ivory was going."

She adds, "But this isn't the first report of illegal walrus hunting on the coast and we suspect they've been doing this for some time."

"What about the bikers?" Shane asks. "We saw them go ashore with the DeGroots earlier in the trip, and if I had to guess who threw Bob Harlowe overboard and who nearly knocked Irene off the boat in Petersburg, it would be them."

"What's more," Robert adds, "they seem to be making a round trip, which is a bit odd for bikers. Generally I'd expect them to be on their way somewhere, not playing tourist."

 "So how can we break this thing open – put some heat on Dorothy and Dutch?" Brad asks. "If we can rattle them enough, maybe we can get them to do something hasty."

"I have an idea," Robert says.

Chapter 19
Peril Strait

The *Matanuska* plows eastward in Peril Strait under blue skies and sunshine. The purser announces on the P.A. system they'll have four hours in Sitka and a bus will be waiting to take passengers into the city.

On the sundeck, tent campers strum their guitars and play cards in thin shirtsleeves. Brad and Irene scan the shoreline with binoculars for bears on the beach. Brad is no longer in the hoodie and no longer keeping his distance from Irene. It's a day for sunglasses and sunscreen. Irene is talking with her friend, the Dutch kid, who asked her earlier to sketch him for his parents.

"Did you see that?" the kid shouts. "There! Right there!"

Brad pivots in time to catch several black-and-white whales breaching a few hundred yards to port. One seems to stand vertically in the water for a moment, its head entirely above the surface, looking around.

"Those are orcas and that's a spy hop," a ship's officer says. It's the mate, headed back to the bridge with a cup of coffee. Several tent-campers from the sundeck get up and gather at the rail now. The Dutch kid points to the spot where the mammals last surfaced.

"They're probably transients or offshores," the officer says. "The northern orca families are seal-hunters and we see them a lot in this stretch. If we encounter any ahead of us we'll slow the ship, give them space and watch the show for a while."

Brad strolls the deck and finds the steward by the rail outside the cafeteria, smoking again.

Throughout this entire trip he has tried to avoid moralizing but today he can't stop himself. "You really should do something about that habit, you know," he says. "Live longer."

"I know," the steward replies. "A few others have pointed it out before you."

"So what is Sitka like? All I know is what I read in Michener's *Alaska* and in Ivan Doig's *The Sea Runners* ages ago."

"Yep. Incredible sea adventure story by Ivan Doig about some Scandinavian indentured servants who escape from New Archangel when the Russian America Company runs Sitka. That's what they called it then – New Archangel. The book is based on a true incident, as you probably remember."

"Yes, I loved that book. Really got me interested in Alaska."

"You know Sitka is where Michener lived when he wrote his masterpiece about Alaska. People say Sitka represents the quintessential Alaska, has a softness and beauty you won't find anywhere else. It will affect you like no other place you've ever been in your life."

"This whole state is such a paradise on Earth. Why would anyone want to wreck it to make a dollar?"

"I ask myself that every day," the steward replies. "People like that, they have no soul."

Brad is thinking. How can he write about something as big and raw and beautiful as this state? He still doesn't know how this story will end. Whether the DeGroots land behind bars or not, he must find the words to convey what greed does to such places and the people who live here. That's one advantage a journalist has over a police officer. The police succeed only when they get their man and win in court. A journalist has other tools if he's skillful enough.

*

In the recliner lounge just in front of the sundeck, Robert and Marie, both in full uniform, find the bikers asleep with shirts over their eyes to block out the bright sun. Robert places a hand on the closer man's shoulder and shakes gently. "Wake up sir please," he says. "Wake up."

The two men grunt, startled, and sit up, blinking at the light, rubbing their faces and registering the uniforms in front of them. In his trooper hat, the stocky Robert is an intimidating figure. Shane, in civvies, backs up Robert and Marie with his Whatcom County Sheriffs Office badge displayed on his belt.

"Robert Yuka, state troopers. This is Marie Martin, US Fish and Wildlife Service, and detective Shane Lindstrom." Robert doesn't mention that Shane is from out of state.

"May we see some identification, please," Robert asks.

The men reach for their wallets in their back pockets. "Is there some problem here?" the larger man asks.

"Just answer my questions, sir," Robert says, his eyes boring a hole in the man's face.

"You are Bulk Larson," Robert declares, nodding to the larger man, and this is "Sieve Larson. Brothers? Both of you live on Lakeway Drive in Bellingham."

"That's right."

Robert hands the men's licenses to Shane, who makes some notes on a yellow legal pad and hands them back.

"And the purpose of your trip?" Robert asks.

"Sightseeing," Bulk says. "Always wanted to see Alaska."

"Seems like you're sleeping through it," Robert observes.

"Well I guess we're night owls," Sieve remarks.

"You were up late a few nights ago when one of your fellow passengers went over the rail."

Bulk looks shocked. "Is that right? Did someone jump?"

"No, I don't think so," Robert says. "You were two of the last people seen with him."

"Who in the world are you talking about?"

"You tell me. You walked out of the bar with him."

"I'm afraid I have no idea who or what you're talking about."

"Would you like to see him again?" Robert asks. "Because he's in Sitka right now as we speak." He omits any mention of Bob Harlowe's condition.

Bulk's jaw hangs open. "Hey, what is this anyway? Are you arresting us?"

"No, not right now."

"Cause if you are, aren't you supposed to read us our rights? I think I'd like a lawyer."

"No need," Robert says. "Just think about whether you want to take the fall for this by yourselves or get on my good side by telling me who you are working for and what you know. I'll be around, but I'm awfully busy. If someone else answers my questions first, I won't have any need to be nice to you anymore."

He adds, "Oh, one other thing. I'm pissed about what you did to one of our female passengers the other night. Really pissed."

*

"That was beautiful," Marie says as the three of them walk out of the recliner lounge. "Let them stew for a few hours."

"Thanks for backing me up with the uniform," he nods to Marie, "and the badge," he nods to Shane. "The show of force sends a message. This boat is suddenly going to feel very small for the DeGroots' and anyone associated with them."

For Brad and Irene on the sundeck, the view gets better and better as the ferry approaches the Sitka terminal at Halibut Point, five miles from town. The ship heads into the first of two narrow channels that shelter it from the open sea. Snow-capped mountains, like canine teeth, tower ahead.

*

"Harlowe is alive," Bulk tells Dorothy and Dutch back at their cabin.

"That's preposterous – not possible," Dutch replies.

"Well that's not what the trooper says."

Bulk fills in Dorothy and Dutch on the threatening visit from the uniformed state trooper, wildlife officer and detective.

"How did all these enforcement officers suddenly appear on the boat?" Dorothy asks. "Jesus, Dutch, you've screwed the pooch. I thought you had everything under control."

"It is," he says. "Our hands are clean. But," turning to Bulk, "we've got to get you and Sieve off the boat. I'll make it well worth your while if you keep your cool and don't say anything."

"The troopers know where we live," Sieve says. "If we go to back to

Bellingham they'll be waiting for us."

"Then let's get you on a floatplane to Hoonah or Angoon. You can lie low and maybe crew on a fishing boat for a while. Lose the beards and biker gear. Drop out of sight till things quiet down."

Dutch advises Bulk and Sieve to take the bus to Sitka with the other passengers as if they're just sightseeing. "Don't take any packs or extra gear that would imply you're leaving the boat. I'll give you some spending money now and send more soon." He opens his wallet and counts out $500, which he gives them along with the phone number of a contact in Sitka who can fly them to one of the smaller communities at Dutch's expense.

At the Sitka terminal Bulk and Sieve walk ashore with a crowd of passengers while Dorothy and Dutch, and Robert, Marie and Shane all watch from the rail.

Three Sitka Police cars, red-and-blue lights flashing, pull into the parking lot and stop in front, behind and beside the bus. Officers get out, hands on their holsters, and approach the crowd. Before the bikers can board the bus, in full view of the ship, police order them aside.

"Hands against the side of the bus and spread your feet," an officer commands the two. His partner frisks Bulk, then Sieve, and handcuffs them behind their backs. An officer escorts Bulk to the first car, opens the back door and pushes his head down as Bulk disappears into the back. Another officer does the same with Sieve, placing him in a separate vehicle.

"What are we charging them with?" Marie asks.

"Nothing," Robert replies. "We can hold them for 24 hours without charges. We'll keep them separate and question them independently. The next few hours will be torture for the DeGroots."

Chapter 20
Sitka

From 500 feet overhead, Nguyen studies the procession of tugs, barges, powerboats and sailing vessels following the Inside Passage north. The drone of the DeHavilland's Stinson engine drowns out everything outside the cabin, as if the whole scene were just a silent movie unfolding in slow motion.

"Change of plans," Nguyen speaks into his headset as the DeHavilland passes Alert Bay on Vancouver Island.

"I want you to drop me at Roche Harbor, not Bellingham. But let's have radio silence, please. I require some discretion."

"Roger. Not a problem. Roche Harbor it is."

FINAL PASSAGE

The DeHavilland drones on. The pilot thinks the Roche Harbor marina and hotel complex on Washington's San Juan Island is an oddly isolated destination for such a humorless passenger traveling alone. Roche Harbor is a favorite layover for boaters and those on a romantic getaway. The Hotel de Haro is known for its historic charm, its flower gardens and dining. Washington State Ferries visit the island several times a day on their inter-island run and also on the international route to and from Vancouver Island, Canada. Other than that, travel is by floatplanes, land-based aircraft and private boats.

*

At the Sitka police station, Bulk Larsen sits with his feet shackled to a table leg in an interview room. A fluorescent tube overhead flickers annoyingly. Robert Yuka enters the room and sits down in a metal folding chair on the other side of the table as Shane and Marie watch through a mirror.

"How do you like Sitka so far?" Robert asks.

"Sucks," Bulk replies.

"The sucking hasn't even started yet. You are what my people call a small fish. I'm looking for a bigger one and I'm very impatient. If you help me, there might still be time to salvage a relationship between us."

"Look, Indian boy, am I charged with something? If I'm not, then I think we're both wasting our time."

"This is going to be more fun than I thought," Robert says. "You are going nowhere until I say so. And right now, I think your little brother in the next room is having some serious second thoughts about whether he wants to take the fall with you."

*

"I'm telling you, you've screwed the pooch!" Dorothy yells at Dutch in the privacy of their cabin. "If those two losers start talking, it's going to lead straight back to us."

"The cops have nothing," Dutch replies. "Bulk has some personal reasons to keep his mouth shut. If Bulk and Sieve start talking it'll be their word against ours. What motive would we have to hire a couple of lowlifes to throw someone off the boat? The smartest thing they can do is keep quiet, because I can implicate them in some other activities they'd like to forget. Nguyen is long gone and they can't trace him. The mushers don't know what they were transporting, nor for whom."

"Well I'd feel a lot better if we weren't cooped up on this boat with three cops for the next three days," Dorothy says.

∗

"What do you think?" Brad asks.

"It's like something from a dream! We don't have anything like this in Stanley," Irene replies as they gaze west at the snowy crater of Mt. Edgecumbe volcano on Kruzof Island, just across from the city. "What a picture postcard scene," she adds as the sun warms them on a blue-sky day.

Brad and Irene are standing on Castle Hill overlooking the harbor, where Tlingit natives once lived before Alexander Baranov seized the hill in the Battle of Sitka. It's also where the first U.S. flag was raised after Alaska became the 49th state.

"It's so odd to suddenly be in a Russian town," Irene says.

"Did you ever read Michener's *Alaska?*" Brad asks.

"I tried. It's huge."

"Parts of it are downright painful, with all the exploitation of natives and wildlife in the fur trade. But it gives a graphic picture of what went on between the Russians and the indigenous peoples, and later with the Americans. In a few hours we can only hit a few of the highlights – the Russian Bishop's House, St. Michael's Cathedral, Totem Park, the raptor center, Sheldon Jackson Museum."

"We'll then I guess you owe me another trip so we spend some real time here," Irene says.

*

A few blocks away, Sieve Larsen sits alone in a police interview room for 45 minutes. The door finally opens and it's Robert Yuka.

"I think your big brother is going to sell you down the river," Robert begins, " . . . which, I'm sorry to say, puts you in a hell of a place. Once I get what I need from him, I won't need to strike any deals with you. Is there anything you'd like to say to get some credit for cooperating? I don't have time to screw around."

"None of what happened with the pilot was my idea," Sieve says. "Those people, the DeGroots, had some leverage over Bulk so he had to do what they told him."

"But you don't know what that leverage was?"

"He never told me."

"And," Yuka asks, "you took part why?"

"How is this going to help me?"

"Tell me something useful about the DeGroots and I'll tell the prosecutor you were a cooperative witness."

*

The DeHavilland circles low over Roche Harbor as the pilot scans the water below for any movement by other float planes or boats that might interfere with his approach. This is a tight spot and he's losing the daylight, but he descends to 50 feet, below tree level, and threads

122

the needle, following the narrow channel between McCracken Point and Pearl Island.

As the DeHavilland rounds Pearl Island, the pilot banks left toward the marina and then slaps the plane down hard, taking one long skip before finding the water again and slowing sharply. The pilot taxis straight ahead toward the float-plane dock, cuts power and lets the aircraft drift while he pops open the door and steps onto the pontoon with a line in his hand. He throws the free end to a Good Samaritan who's watching from the dock. The guy pulls the plane alongside and loops the line smartly back and forth around a cleat.

"Much obliged for that assist," the pilot declares.

With the engine now quiet, Nguyen is on his cell phone, speaking in Vietnamese. He completes the call, hangs up and announces, "I'll wait here with the plane. Some friends of mine will be here to pick me up in a moment."

*

"It was never the plan to throw that guy overboard," Sieve says. "We were just going to put the fear of god in him. When Bulk folded him over the rail and gave him that push, I never saw that coming. That's some serious shit."

"Do you think that was Bulk's intention all along – to put him over the rail?"

"I don't know. Dutch told us the guy needed to shut up because he was talking too much, to the wrong people. I thought we were going to hurt him. I didn't hear anything about killing him."

"So what are the DeGroots up to that requires silencing people?" Robert asks.

"That's their business, not ours," Sieve says.

"So you came all this way, working for someone, and you don't even know what business they're in? You think I believe that?"

"The money is good. Sometimes it's better not to know more than that. They run an airline. I think maybe they do some shit that may not be completely legal."

*

At the floatplane dock in Roche Harbor a powerboat approaches with two Asian men aboard. They shout to Nguyen in Vietnamese and he shouts back, gesturing toward the cargo hold of the DeHavilland.

One of the men gets out and opens the hold, and hands a bag to his colleague on the boat. They spend several minutes transferring bags and stowing them below deck. Nguyen joins them in the cockpit of the boat and it roars off in the direction of Anacortes.

At the Hotel de Haro, a man with binoculars watches it all. In the fading daylight he can't see details very well. He puts down the binoculars and reaches for his iPad, and scrolls back through his email and finds the one he remembers, and starts to punch buttons on his cell phone.

*

Irene is just settling into her sketching in the forward observation lounge as the *Matanuska* pulls away from the Sitka dock. Dorothy DeGroot enters the lounge and walks over to her.

"Dorothy!" Irene greets enthusiastically. "How did you like Sitka?"

"We didn't go."

"Oh no!" Irene replies. "You missed the highlight of this entire trip."

Chapter 21
Southbound

"We got enough out of Sieve Larsen to charge him and his brother with murder," Robert tells Brad, Shane and Marie back in Shane's cabin. "But we don't have much on Dorothy and Dutch – just Sieve's statement that the DeGroots wanted the pilot silenced, not necessarily killed."

"We need to get Bulk talking," Shane says.

"What we really need is the ivory and the guy who bought it," Marie adds. "What do we have on C. Nguyen?"

"There's no such person," Robert says.

"What about the pilot who flew him out of Juneau?"

"We have almost no way to trace him unless we can get Dorothy and Dutch to tell us," Robert says.

"Well the plane had to go somewhere," Brad says.

"My money's on Bellingham or Oak Harbor, since DeGroot has connections in both of those places," Shane says. "But a lot of float planes fly to Kenmore on Lake Washington. We've alerted operators in all those locations to let us know of arriving DeGroot aircraft.

"They could be there already," Robert says. "The trouble is, a float plane equipped with a wheel kit can land on either water or a runway

. . . or even a good, private dirt strip if they have one. That's a lot of ground to cover."

"We need a lucky break," Marie says.

"Well let's all get a few hours' sleep and come at this hard in the morning," Robert suggests. "Marie, do you have a few minutes for a walk around the deck to discuss some strategy?"

Bingo, Brad thinks. He remembers how it feels to start something new.

The sun is setting behind the *Matanuska* as it plows eastward, away from Sitka and toward its next stops of Petersburg and Wrangell. Brad wonders what tomorrow will bring.

He's happy for Robert and Marie, but has a bad feeling that the criminal investigation has come down to lucky breaks. The DeGroots have a history of covering their tracks just well enough to avoid prosecution.

That's certainly true in the murder of his journalism school classmate, Bella Morelli, whose body washed ashore under Whidbey Island's Deception Pass Bridge. Bella's apparent suicide protects the DeGroots' real estate investments from collapse if her articles should nudge the Navy to pull its Growler aircraft off Whidbey Island. The DeGroots silence Bella before she can do that, but Brad finishes the job with his own national expose after Bella's death.

Now it's clear the DeGroots are established in a new scam. They have some colossal bad luck in putting themselves in the same place as a boatload of investigators. But they distance themselves just enough from the murder of pilot Bob Harlowe to avoid answering for that as well, unless Bulk Larsen comes clean or his brother Sieve has more to say.

More troubling is the disappearance of the walrus ivory driving this whole investigation and the buyer who is right under their noses but slips away. Brad thinks the ivory is likely bound for a large metropolitan area with an international community, such as Seattle or Vancouver, where an Asian trafficker can easily disappear. But unless they can trace the flight and the pilot who transported the contraband south, the trail is cold. Wildlife agents have no luck locating the two hunters who deliver the ivory to Haines. They, too, are long gone.

So as a journalist with a national platform, what can he do? He can shine a spotlight on the illegal walrus hunts and those who transport the contraband, but it's way short of what he really wants – to put Dot and Dutch behind bars for what's left of their lives.

Marie is right – they need a break – but Brad thinks they're at the stage where they're going to have to force it. He hopes that's Robert's plan, as well.

Chapter 22
Wrangell

Wrangell seems sleepy to Brad in the morning mist as the *Matanuska* arrives for a brief stop. The boat must slip in and out of this port almost unnoticed by the locals, he thinks.

This is a wet place and he's in a mellow mood. He smiles as he recalls the words of his Aunt Helen, a young school teacher whose first job after graduation in the 1930s was right here in Wrangell, of all places.

"I arrived in a gray town, on a gray day, on a gray boat."

He wonders what people do in a place like this with so many dreary days. His Aunt Helen landed a job as organist for the large Presbyterian Church here as soon as she hit town. Brad remembers from his reading that the church has a rich history as the first protestant church of any denomination in Wrangell, having been founded by S. Hall Young, an associate of Sheldon Jackson.

Young, in turn, was a friend of the naturalist John Muir, and together they explored much of the nearby Stikine River and the surrounding area.

Shortly after Brad's aunt arrived here and began serving as Presbyterian organist, the Catholic and Episcopal ministers heard about her and staggered the hours of their services so she could play for them, too. They were all located on Church Street, which strikes Brad as curious. Maybe that's a holdover of the Sheldon Jackson legacy.

There's a Cow Alley, too, but he doesn't know the story behind that.

More significant, he knows, is the native presence in this place, which goes back thousands of years. Tlingit peoples migrated down the Stikine River long before recorded history, and the river remained their highway to the interior. The many petroglyphs in the area are evidence of their ancient occupation.

Russians arrived here in 1811 and took up fur trading with the natives. Hudson's Bay Company followed, and later the Americans.

As Brad absorbs all these thoughts he realizes he slept through Petersburg and the narrows during the night. This must mean he's falling into the round-the-clock rhythm of ferry life. Only two cars wait in the holding area this morning to board for the trip south.

Sirens in the distance alert Brad that someone's morning across town is not starting as well as his own. But the sirens grow louder, and soon he sees the flashing red-and-blue lights of two police cars and a medical aid van heading straight for the ferry. One police vehicle stops in the holding area and the other follows the aid van right onto the boat.

What the . . .? Is this something Robert and Marie cooked up?

Brad tries to make sense of it. He heads for the stairwell to the car deck but finds it blocked. Irene's friend, the Dutch kid, is standing there, listening.

"One, two . . . clear!" Brad hears. "Again. One, two . . . clear!"

"What's happening?" Brad asks.

"I think some guy had a heart attack," the Dutch kid says. "They're working on him down at the bottom of the stairs."

"Any idea who it is?"

"Some older guy coming up the stairs. I started down to see if I could go ashore but the crew stopped me. I didn't get a very good look. Whoever he is, he probably won't be going with us on the boat today."

Brad races through the possibilities. "Older" to a kid could be almost anyone. Could it be Robert or Shane? The kid didn't get a good look. My god, maybe Dutch DeGroot. He has to be feeling stress.

Or is the whole dramatic scene a diversion?

Brad is listening intently when he feels a hand come to rest on his shoulder.

"Ready to go to work?" It's Robert Yuka.

"Oh, Robert!" Brad begins. "I'm relieved to see you."

"The feeling's mutual," Robert replies. "I heard it was an old guy."

"Thanks," Brad replies with a smirk. "What the heck is going on?"
"I don't have a clue. But I hope it makes the DeGroots hearts skip a few beats to see police cars and flashing lights."

"So this is none of your doing?"

"No. I swear it isn't.

"How was your walk with Marie last night?"

Robert smiles. "Productive."

"You're not telling me much."

"Us natives aren't real chatty."

Just then Brad notices Shane coming their way.

"Good," Brad says. "Whoever is lying at the bottom of the stairs, it's not one of us."

"Yeah, and I have some other good news," Shane says. "We had a sighting of the DeGroot plane last night. An FAA employee from Bellingham noticed it tied to a float at Roche Harbor, unloading bags onto a powerboat. The plane took off before dark and the powerboat left with three men aboard as soon as the bags were loaded, but at least we can narrow the search a bit now."

"Do we have a description of the boat?" Brad asks.

"Just the general appearance. It was getting dark and the guy couldn't make out any registration numbers."

Brad rests his hand pensively on his chin and looks at the floor.

"Why the San Juans? What's the point of that?"

"Mr. Nguyen didn't think we'd be looking there," Shane replies. "Wherever he's taking the ivory, we now know can get there from

Roche Harbor by boat."

"That's a lot of territory," Brad says.

"It could be some nearby town like Anacortes or Port Townsend, but could just as easily be Victoria if he's really sneaky and wants to escape U.S. jurisdiction by running to Canada. It could also be a private home with a dock on any of the islands. There are some pretty secluded, upscale estates in the San Juans – movie stars, corporate executives."

Shane continues, "I've got the Coast Guard and San Juan County Sheriff looking for the boat but we don't have much to go on, and they had all night to get somewhere."

"So what's next?" Brad asks.

"Marie and I think it's time to split up Dorothy and Dutch and give them something to sweat about. See if one of them is ready to jump ship on the other," Robert says.

"That would be Dorothy," Irene remarks. "She's the brains in that marriage, and she's too smart to go down in flames with Dutch."

"Then I think we should catch her when Dutch isn't around – plant some ideas and give her time to think," Robert says.

Chapter 23
Ketchikan

The *Matanuska* pulls into Ketchikan in the late morning for a four-hour layover. It's the final Alaska stop of this trip that will end in Bellingham at 8 a.m. Friday. The steward tells Brad and Shane the boat will likely be pretty quiet here. There's always a big exodus of passengers downtown to see the historic red light district on Creek Street and take the tram up to the restaurant at Cape Fox Lodge. "Good place to try someone else's cuisine," he laughs.

Creek Street sounds fun to Brad. He suggests to Irene they catch a city bus downtown and give Robert and Marie some space to interview Dorothy.

As they wait to disembark, Brad notices a Ketchikan City Police SUV parked at the landing. As soon as the ship is secure, two officers come aboard – one male, one female, both in black uniforms.

*

Dorothy and Dutch are startled by the knock on their cabin door. Dutch opens it to find two Ketchikan police officers.

"Oh for the love of god," he declares.

The officers introduce themselves and show identification, and explain they'd like Dutch to accompany them downtown to answer some questions. "We'll get you back before the ship sails."

FINAL PASSAGE

"This is highly irregular," Dutch protests.

"Your airline, DeGroot Air, flies through Ketchikan and we'd just like to understand your business a little better," one of the officers explains. "We think you can help clear up some questions we have in connection with an investigation into some illegal hunting activities."

DeGroot accompanies them with obvious reluctance.

Moments later, Robert Yuka and Marie Martin find Dorothy in the forward observation lounge, reading *The Passenger*, by Lisa Lutz.

"Is that pretty good?" Robert asks.

"Oh you know, sergeant, it's a psychological thriller. I'm all for that."

"I like psychological stories, too," Marie says. "But as long as we've caught you here, could we talk a moment? We understand your husband has gone downtown with some city police officers for an hour or two. Sergeant Yuka and I thought we might have a word with you in private while he's gone."

"I can't for the life of me imagine why you're interested in either one of us."

"Humor us a little, Mrs. DeGroot," Robert interjects. "We'll explain. The cafeteria is pretty quiet right now with so many passengers ashore. Maybe we can find a peaceful corner and snag a cup of coffee."

They walk to the stern and get their coffee. Dorothy's cup rattles on its saucer as she walks to the table and sits down across from Robert and Marie.

"I think you know, Mrs. DeGroot, that this little cat and mouse game is getting pretty serious for you and Dutch," Robert begins.

"Is there a cat-and-mouse game?"

He continues, "We have two accomplices of yours in custody already who say your husband ordered the murder of one of your employees, Robert Harlowe. We know you transported and sold walrus ivory on board this ship, and we know who bought it, and are closing in on his location right now. We know your company brokered the hunt for that ivory and that one of your airplanes flew it from Juneau to Washington. We'll be talking with the pilot just as soon as we can chase him down."

"Jesus, sergeant. That's a lot to just lay on somebody."

"It *is* a lot, Mrs. DeGroot. I would not want to be in your shoes. Which is why I thought you might like to get ahead of this a little rather than take the whole fall with Dutch."

"Just what exactly are you suggesting?"

"I'm suggesting you should tell us what you know voluntarily so I can tell the prosecutor you cooperated with us."

"Well if that isn't the lamest thing. If you're arresting me I think it would be prudent to call a lawyer."

"No," Robert says. "We're not arresting you at this time – just having a conversation."

"Is that how you do things, sergeant – turn spouses against each other? Dutch and I have been through a lot in 30 years of marriage and been very successful. When you've accomplished as much as we have in business and politics a lot of people want to tear you down. That's just how it is."

"It depends on what you do to get ahead."

"Well I scratched my way up from the bottom, sergeant. My parents were dirt-poor turkey farmers on Whidbey Island back before World War II when that whole farm economy went belly up on the island. I know a lot about boom and bust – mostly the bust."

"I've heard the story," Robert says. "You married Dutch, a guy with ambition, and together you rode the real estate boom fueled by almost continuous expansion of the U.S. Navy presence on Whidbey Island. And you rode the political boom as well."

"It was smart business," Dorothy says. "And then along comes this East Coast reporter, this Italian woman, who blows the whole thing up. Actually, she commits suicide before she can finish what she started, but then your friend Shane and this other reporter, Brad Haraldsen, take up her cause and spook the Navy into pulling back. The two of them destroy our real estate business. So much for the economy of Whidbey Island but that's not enough, and suddenly now we are totally the victims of massive injustice, and still they aren't satisfied. I'm sorry but DeGroot Air is all we've got now."

"That's a heart-rending story, Mrs. DeGroot, but let's get back to the here and now – a dead pilot, one of your husband's employees, two thugs who throw that pilot overboard, an illegal walrus hunt, and a load of ivory that DeGroot Air flies from Juneau to Washington. I might also add we have multiple witnesses who see the buyer in your company."

"This is a small boat on a week-long voyage, so we are all spending time in one-another's company," Dorothy counters. "I don't know anything about any thugs or a dead pilot. If somebody transported something illegal on my husband's airline without his knowledge, that's a bone you need to pick with the passenger, not us."

"Fine," Robert says. "Think about my offer, but don't think too long. The net is closing fast. If someone else sings first, I won't have much need for anything you can add."

*

Dorothy is back in the forward observation lounge, reading her thriller when Dutch returns two hours later.

"What a load of bullshit!" he exclaims. "They've got nothing – absolutely nothing. That was the biggest waste of time I've ever seen."

"So what did they ask you?" Dorothy inquires.

"Just the most inane questions. 'How long have you flown through Ketchikan? Which float facilities do you use and how do you reimburse the owner? How often? How many passengers per month? How do you book reservations? Where do you fly to? Do you screen your passengers as to the purpose of their travel, and so on?'

"Honestly, it didn't make any sense. They were just fishing blind, I guess."

Chapter 24
Friday Harbor, Washington

Sheriff Dave Anderson sips his grande latte at the Bean Café in Friday Harbor. The coffee helps him think. It is a sissy drink, he knows, but it goes down smoothly, unlike the black coffee in his office. And, along with the muffin he orders too, it helps get his 70-year-old bones moving in the morning. He doesn't sleep that well anymore.

The email from his old friend Shane Lindstrom is on his mind. The Bellingham detective, formerly from neighboring Island County, emails Anderson from the Alaska Ferry for help in finding a boat that left Roche Harbor around dusk last night, possibly headed for a shoreline home in the San Juans.

Anderson happens to like Shane and doesn't have much respect for the guy who fired him. That whole Island County political scene strikes him as corrupt. Too much Navy money pouring into the community. Too easy for special interests to pull the strings of the economy as well as local government. All those noisy Growler aircraft are a plague on the peaceful San Juan Islands, too.

Shane's request interests Anderson a little more than some because the subject is suspected of smuggling raw walrus ivory, and is sought by a federal wildlife officer. Parts of Anderson's county are within the San Juan Islands National Wildlife Refuge, and his own daughter is with the agency. Any time he can help nail one of these wildlife creeps, it's especially satisfying. Islanders feel protective of the natural paradise in which they live. Anderson's neighbors are the most progressive environmentalists in the entire Puget Sound basin.

Anderson and a handful of deputies serve a predominantly rural population of 16,000 spread heavily across four principal islands and sporadically across dozens of smaller ones close to an international boundary. Some of the residences are the very private, gated, upscale estates of wealthy absentee owners and seasonal residents. Winter and summer bring wide swings in the population and workload for his office.

Policing these islands is an impossible assignment, especially with all the break-ins and vandalism of unoccupied homes and summer cabins. The county's shape is the most convoluted in Washington with an intricate shoreline, limited road network, limited services, limited ferries, limited police staffing, too many cars and one of the state's smallest law-enforcement budgets. As is true of county police everywhere, Anderson accomplishes more through local knowledge and networking than by patrolling. He's lived here a long time – knows a lot of people.

And Anderson would like a high-profile win. A decade ago, the San Juan County sheriff's department is humiliated by Colton Harris-Moore, the teenage "Barefoot Bandit" from neighboring Island County who steals several airplanes and boats on Orcas and San Juan islands and breaks into dozens of homes, businesses and summer cabins, leaving a rich trail of clues, even *planting* clues and mocking the police.

His predecessor in the department never connects the dots – never realizes who the criminal even is, despite a pattern of clues that links him to a long history of similar property crimes in Island County, and the department fails repeatedly to catch him. That distinction falls to police in the Bahamas after Harris-Moore crosses the country in a stolen airplane and crashes it in their waters.

Shane's email says the suspect is Asian, possibly Vietnamese. That's a place to start. If the powerboat that left Roche Harbor was headed for a home in the San Juans, the sheriff can narrow his search to those with a dock, float or boathouse that can accommodate a powerboat. The county treasurer can help him with properties owned under Asian names.

He guesses that if the suspect is a person of means who owns an upscale boat, he might need a good marine mechanic from time to time. And he might also frequent the better Asian restaurants or order an Asian meal to go. Several restaurants on San Juan, Orcas and Lopez islands serve Asian cuisine. He and his deputies on the neighboring islands will make some inquiries. They'll also check with their contacts at the state ferry system regarding any unusual powerboats they encountered the previous evening on the inter-island run.

It might all lead nowhere, but somebody, somewhere, saw something and somebody knows the mysterious Asian. If he lives in San Juan County, Anderson intends to be the one who finds him.

Chapter 25
B.C. Coast

"That went pretty well, don't you think?" Robert asks Marie as they sit alone in the *Matanuska* bar.

"Very well," she says. "Dorothy is teetering on the brink."

"Let's see where she's at in the morning."

They sit in awkward silence. Marie shakes her ponytail as if it's annoying her. "I need to wash my hair," she declares. Robert takes a sip of his beer. Finally, he begins, "I've been wanting to ask you some things."

Marie fidgets and stares at her nails. "Okay."

"Personal stuff."

"Okay."

There's a pause. She adds, "Sorry, I'm not good at this. There's some stuff I want to ask you, too."

"Okay, you first," Robert says.

"Are you a kayaker?"

"You're kidding? I'm an Indian."

"Sorry. It just that I really like kayaking."

"I can handle a boat," Robert assures her. "Is that your best shot?"

"Your turn," Marie says, blushing. "Does it seem warm in here? Sorry, I think I have rosacea or something."

"Yeah, I see that. I'm going to get right to it, do you eat seal meat."

"*Absolutely* not."

"So was that a maybe?"

"No way. Over my dead body."

"Ok, leave yourself some wiggle room. I don't eat lutefisk, that foul stuff your people dragged over from Norway."

"Well neither do I. Tuna fish. I eat tuna if it contains enough chopped sweet pickles."

"Yeah, me too, if somebody else makes it."

"So let's go back to seal meat," Marie asks. "Just how often do you eat it?"

"Only on ceremonial occasions."

"Tell me about your parents," Marie asks, suddenly serious.

"Like what?"

"What do they do? What kind of people are they?"

"Dad is no longer living. He was the village safety officer. Mom raised us kids – my sister and me – and teaches school. It is a dry village but there are still plenty of drunks, and that was Dad's biggest problem. They raised us to study hard and go easy on alcohol. How about your parents?"

"Military – straight arrow all the way," Marie says, "and I'm a chip off the old block."

"Must be a heckuva block," Robert muses aloud. "Is it a happy marriage?"

"Pretty much. They have their differences but I think both have given the marriage their best, and of course they want good things for me. They dragged me as a kid all over the wilderness, camping and fishing. Taught me a lot about wildlife and wilderness skills."

"Only child?"

"Yeah. Mom nearly died in childbirth and they didn't want to take that risk again. It was always important to me to do well and make my parents proud."

"I know the feeling. I need to tell you something about that."

"Yes?"

"You know how it is in the villages – guys get drunk and go off into the night on their snowmobiles, never to be seen again?"

"Yeah."

"That's how Dad died," Robert says, tearing up. He is fighting now to stay composed and choke out the words. "I mean he . . . he didn't get drunk but he . . . died . . . trying to find a drunk and save his life. He went out into a storm looking for this guy."

Robert stares at his glass and pauses to pull himself together. "Helicopter found his snowmobile broken down a couple days later and Dad didn't make it. That's when I decided I wanted to be a trooper."

"Oh Robert," Marie says, looking across the table with her mouth open. She stands and opens her arms to him. He gets up and wraps his arms around her. She is shaking. He rubs her back.

"Are you ok?" he asks.

"I haven't hugged anyone in a long time," she blubbers into his ear. She's all teared up, too.

He finds her mouth and kisses the salty tears rolling down her face.

"I'm sorry," he says. "I don't know what I am thinking. Is that ok?"

"Yeah," she replies.

Chapter 26
Bella Bella

"Are you feeling homesick yet?" Brad asks.

"Are you kidding?" comes the reply from Irene's bunk. She puts down her book. "Having too much fun. But I'd like to sew up this DeGroot case and it's tough to live a week without a dog."

"Sew up? Listen to you, talking like a hardened cop," Brad remarks. "If you really miss Bear and Ida, I'm surprised you haven't buddied up to that Terry guy who sits out on the deck with the service dog."

"I sketched him – actually the dog. And I might have slipped the dog a couple of bacon strips," she replies, picking up her book again.

"Were did you get bacon?"

"Where do you think?" Irene replies.

"The steward says it's a scam."

"What's a scam?"

"The service dog," Brad says. "Terry can see just fine. He just pretends he has vision loss so he can have the dog with him in his cabin. He doesn't need those dark glasses, either."

"Clever," Irene replies, putting the book down again.

"Happens all the time, according to the steward. The crew can't do anything about it. If somebody puts a vest on their dog and says it's a service dog, they have to let the dog hang out on the passenger decks."

"I'll remember that next time you bring me on this boat." Irene picks up her book again. Neither of them speaks for a moment.

"I called home," Brad adds.

"You did *what?*" Irene asks, putting down her book.

"I called Bolivar."

"We agreed we weren't going to do that this week. Besides, there's no cell signal on this boat."

"There is at Bella Bella." The words are out before Brad has time to catch himself. Why is there a town named after his old girlfriend times two? He tries not to say "Bella" too much in Irene's presence, since Bella was his long-ago lover and the reason he got involved in the whole DeGroot matter in the first place. He's just said it twice.

"You dirty dog," Irene declares, reaching back for her pillow and throwing it across at Brad's bunk.

"It was an impulse decision. I had the phone in my hand and thought, 'I wonder if there's a signal here. Who can I call?'"

"Right. Sure."

"So aren't you curious?" Brad asks.

"About what?"

"Bear and Idaho." Bear is Irene's big German Shepherd and Idaho is Bella's orphaned Golden Retriever. After Bella's death, Brad takes Idaho back to the ranch to live out her days as Bear's girlfriend. Actually, as his wife. The wedding is the idea of a friend of Irene's –

to make Ida an honest dog by performing a little ceremony.

"Ok, I'll bite," Irene says. "How is everyone?"

"They're doing just fine, according to Bolivar. He's been mending fence and doing some fishing every day, and the dogs like the routine. But he says they they'll be glad to see you and go back to living on the couch."

"I'm surprised Bolivar hasn't spent this whole week at Mountain Village Resort in Stanley, having breakfast and spinning stories with his Basque friends," Irene remarks, picking up her book again.

"You left him in charge," Brad replies. "He takes his job very seriously and wants to impress you. This is his big moment."

"I'm sure," Irene says, putting down her book again. "I think he has a crush on that cute waitress at the inn."

"Who's that?"

"Danielle."

"That's right. So when we get home," Brad continues, "be sure to compliment him on how well he kept everything going."

"He knows. We have a thing, Bolivar and me. But what's happening with the DeGroots."

"Robert and Marie are up to something."

"I know but are they working on the case?"

A knock at the door interrupts them. Brad is surprised because of the early hour. "Hang on a second," he yells, reaching for his jeans. He opens the door to find Shane.

"Come in," Brad says. "I hope this is good."

"It is. My friend the San Juan County Sheriff has narrowed the search for Nguyen a bit. He talked to the mate on last night's inter-island ferry and learned they passed a powerboat off Shaw Island that was running east with no lights. That's highly unusual – both the late hour and the failure to display lights."

"So what does this tell us?" Brad asks.

"We can take Victoria off the table, and also Port Townsend and San Juan Island itself, and the whole Olympic Peninsula. If that's the boat we think it is, it was headed for Anacortes or Bellingham, or one of the islands closer to Anacortes. The sheriff feels like he has a good fighting chance on this one. He has put out a lot of feelers."

"Seems like a needle in a haystack," Brad remarks.

"Not if you know the area like Anderson does. If the boat was headed for a destination somewhere in Anderson's county, he'll find it sooner or later."

"Well if it takes much longer, we'll be back in Bellingham in time to get in on the fun," Brad remarks.

"I'm way ahead of you on that. It wouldn't be the worst thing that could happen."

Chapter 27
San Juan Island

The FedEx truck rolls off the ferry at 8:30 a.m. and heads for its first stop of the morning at the sheriff's office. The driver pulls up in front, beeps twice, then wrestles a box from the stack behind him.

"This looks pretty interesting," he remarks as he comes through the door with a big white box and plants it in the center of the sheriff's desk.

"That's what I've been waiting for," Anderson replies. "I'm going out on a limb ordering this. It may be an old man's folly but I've been wanting to play around with one of these for a long time."

His dispatcher Joan already is on her feet for a closer look. She studies the picture on the box, shaking her head. "Boys and their toys," she smirks.

Anderson fires a warning shot before she can say another word. "Before you even ask, Joan, I paid for this from my own damn pocket, not the county budget. My wife doesn't know and I'd like to keep it that way."

"You know me," Joan says. "Hear nothing. See nothing."

"That's what worries me."

"So are you getting a divorce?"" she asks.

"What makes you ask?"

"Cause men do stuff like this when they're finally free – buy a motorcycle or whatever. But with that bald head and belly, I'm not sure you want to jump back into the dating pool."

"I'm out of here," the FedEx driver says, heading for the door. "But let me just point out a guy could have a lot of fun with that."

"Meaning what?" Joan asks.

"Meaning use your imagination."

Anderson slits the "Fragile" tape on the top of the box with a letter opener and pulls back the flaps. He removes the owner's manual and the quick start guide, and several large chunks of solid foam insulation, exposing four mechanical legs and four little propellers.

"Hold onto the box, will you Joan, while I lift this out."

"She's a beauty," Joan exclaims.

Anderson sets the contraption on his desk, then remembers something and runs out the door after the driver.

"Hey, Bill," he calls. "Do you get around to Orcas and Lopez?"

"Yeah, I handle those routes sometimes."

"Do you deliver to any Asian households?"

"A few. There are several around Eastsound. Everyone out here shops on the Internet. I pick up a lot of outgoing from a place way out in the sticks on the east side of Orcas, behind Mt. Constitution."

"Do you remember the name?"

"Phan or Tran, something like that," he says. "Nice house but isolated. Lots of security – chain link fences, cameras and such. But that's not unusual with the nicer estates."

"On the water?"

"Yeah."

"Ok, thanks."

Returning to the office, the sheriff dials his Orcas deputy. "Get out your best maps and work up a list ASAP of waterfront homes that have boat docks in East Sound and the entire eastern shoreline of Orcas Island. Google Earth will help you find the properties that have boats and docks."

"That's going to be a long list."

"I know. We're going to narrow it down eventually to an Asian household with a dock, float or boathouse that can handle a powerboat. Don't go knocking on any doors – just get me the locations and names. Pay particular attention to an upscale property owned by a Phan or Tran – that's a tip from the FedEx driver. If you have time, cross-check with local restaurants that serve Asian food. They may have names and recollections of Asian customers who live in the area."

Anderson then calls two other deputies at their homes and requests a similar review of shoreline households on Lopez and Shaw islands.

He grabs a walkie talkie and attaches it to his belt, then picks up the contraption on his desk.

"I'll be over at the park for a few minutes," he tells Joan. "Call if you need me. I've got to see if I can fly this thing."

"Isn't there a battery to charge?"

"The Quick Start guide says it's mostly charged. I should have enough juice for a short test."

FINAL PASSAGE

*

On the *Matanuska,* the soft light of dawn floods across the water beneath a low cloud deck and bathes the forested shore in golden hues. The greens and blues are intense. Marie stands by the rail, inhaling the brisk morning air. She watches several dolphins break the surface repeatedly, arching just above the surface and then disappearing again so quickly she wonders if she really saw them. She hasn't felt this happy in years – the water, the beauty, the beginnings of romance . . .

"Penny for your thoughts," a female voice asks from behind.

Marie turns. It's Dorothy DeGroot.

"Just happy thoughts," Marie says.

"You're a lucky girl. Mine aren't so happy. Is that trooper friend of yours around?"

"I can find him. Hang on here and I'll be right back."

Marie heads back to the staterooms and knocks on Robert's door. "Dorothy is ready to talk. She's out on the deck by the cafeteria, port side."

"I'm on my way."

Marie hurries back. Dorothy is gone. Did she step inside? Marie starts looking with some urgency. People seem preoccupied and crew members look concerned.

Suddenly, alarms ring and the ship leans into a sharp turn, the most violent maneuver of the voyage. Crew members run to emergency stations and to the winch for the motorized rescue boat. The ship continues its turn till it is headed back in its own wake.

The loudspeaker blares, "Crew, prepare for rescue operation. Passengers, please stand back and give the crew plenty of room to work."

The steward dons a life vest.

"What's happening?" Marie asks.

"I think we just lost someone overboard."

"How did that happen?"

"I don't know. A woman – quite tall. Someone said she just jumped."

"That isn't possible," Marie says.

Robert joins her. Brad, Shane and Irene come running as well, realizing the ship is in full emergency response to something.

"Why would she jump?" Marie asks. "She was facing a relatively light sentence if she turned evidence against Dutch." Suddenly Marie feels a wave of unexpected sadness for this hard-hearted woman who used political power to control her opponents and probably conspired in the murder of at least two people.

"I don't know," Robert says. "We need to find the person who saw her jump, if that's really what happened."

Minutes pass as the ship closes on a patch of color in its own wake. It's Dorothy's red blouse, and Marie can see Dorothy's arms swinging back and forth in the air. The ship veers off to the side and reduces speed so its wake doesn't swamp her. The rescue boat splashes into the water alongside the ferry and two crewmen in vests start the outboard and head for the object in the water.

Marie watches as the rescue boat reaches the red object and the men lean over the side and struggle to pull it into the raft. Passengers watch with binoculars and snap pictures with their cameras. This is not a Facebook show, Marie thinks. This is someone's life in the balance.

"They've got to save her," Marie says. "We need her testimony."

An officer's walkie-talkie nearby crackles with static.

"We have her. She's breathing but hypothermic," a voice on the radio says. "Spitting up water. Very cold. Blue. Shaking badly but we're wrapping her in blankets."

Dutch DeGroot appears on deck. "What's going on?" he asks a cook from the cafeteria.

"Woman overboard," the cook says, and then adds, "I'm afraid it's your wife."

"How did it happen?"

"She just went over the rail."

"Nooooo," Dutch wails. "That is not possible."

The steward overhears the exchange and comes to Dutch's side. "I'm afraid it is," he tells him. "We think we got to her in time. We hope so."

The *Matanuska* now sits dead in the water. The rescue craft pulls alongside its blue hull and crewmen from the vehicle deck open a side door and lift Dorothy aboard, followed by the raft crew. Robert and Marie watch her disappear into the vessel and can no longer see what's happening. Dutch wants to go to her side. The steward tells him, "Give us some time to stabilize her. Those raft guys are fire department EMTs at home – they know what to do."

Below decks, the first mate directs them to a warm cabin. Crew strip off Dorothy's wet clothing and wrap her in wool blankets, topped by an electric blanket, and begin the slow, deliberate process of stabilizing her, all while watching her pulse and blood pressure.

"What's happening?" Marie asks the steward. "What is her condition?"

"She's alive but the next hour will be critical," the steward says. "I've participated in these rescues before. Typically, body temperature continues to go down at first, before it starts to respond to being warmed."

On the bridge, the captain is on the radio to Canadian authorities in Port Hardy, Vancouver Island.

"What happens now?" Marie asks the steward, who is removing his floatation vest.

"I think that's what the captain is deciding right now," he says. "Generally we call for a Coast Guard helo to evacuate the patient to a hospital. The nearest is Port Hardy. In this case I don't know. She's been through a lot. It may be better to do what we can here, without winching her up on a spinning gurney to a helicopter that is blowing a downdraft on her at 150 miles an hour."

Marie turns to Robert. "We can't lose her to Port Hardy. If she leaves this ship and ends up in Canada, we may never learn what she knows in time to catch our suspect."

"Agreed. I'll do what I can with the captain." He turns and heads for the bridge. "Talk to people," he calls over his shoulder. "See if you can find someone who saw her go overboard. If Dutch is behind this, we've got to know."

Brad, Shane, Robert and Marie turn to the crowd and begin making inquiries. Several people report that Dorothy simply looked both ways, climbed up on the rail and jumped feet first into the water. Witnesses rushed to the stern and looked for her. She was under water for a time, then reappeared on the surface behind the ship.

*

"There isn't any Phan or Tran on Orcas Island," the Eastsound deputy reports by phone to Sheriff Anderson. "But I think I identified that house the FedEx driver mentioned."

"Yeah?"

"The property was sold to a Hoang."

"Recently?"

"It turned over about a year ago. The other Asian households on Orcas are more long term and the families are well known – kids in the schools and active in the arts, all that."

"Okay," the sheriff says. "That's helpful. I need to hear from Lopez and Shaw, and then we'll see where we stand."

On a whim he calls a boat mechanic in Eastsound. "You do any powerboat work for a Mr. Hoang?" he asks.

"Say that again," the mechanic asks. The sheriff repeats it.

No," the mechanic says, laughing. "I think I'd remember that name."

"Anyone else Asian?"

"There is one guy. I don't like him much – not very friendly – but the boat is sweet and he pays cash.

"Where does this guy live?" the sheriff asks.

"No idea. I never see anything with an address."

"Name?"

"Let me think a sec. Nguyen."

Chapter 28
Canadian Waters

The *Matanuska* is under way again, plowing south toward Port Hardy and the northern tip of Vancouver Island. Passengers are suddenly somber now, talking among themselves in small groups in quieter tones. Irene finds her California friends, Jack and Alta, in the forward observation lounge.

"That's something you don't expect to see," Jack remarks. "Or that you hope you'll never see. Have you heard whether that lady is going to survive?"

"As far as I know she is improving," Irene says.

"I know you've been keeping an eye on those people for some time," Jack says. "Just promise me we'll get the story someday of what really happened on this boat."

"You will – soon," Irene says. "Things are falling into place."

The captain decides against an unscheduled stop in Port Hardy to transfer Dorothy. They'll push on, spend the night sailing in the lee of the immense Vancouver Island, and arrive in Bellingham on schedule at 8 a.m. The captain informs Robert Yuka he has decided against hospitalizing Mrs. DeGroot.

"She's improving, temperature coming up, and our medics are on top of her care. I understand Mr. DeGroot is asking to see her."

"You can't let that happen," Robert tells him. "We're at a very delicate point in a criminal investigation. We believe she was preparing to turn evidence against her husband. He may already suspect this, and if he does, she could be in grave danger if he gains access to her."

Robert adds, "All it would take is a few minutes alone with her, with a pillow. He wouldn't leave much evidence."

"Then we'll keep her isolated on the lower deck and tell her husband she's out of danger but not strong enough yet for a visitor. I'll have someone with her at all times."

"However," Robert continues, "Marie Martin and I need some time with her as soon as possible."

*

"So how's the new toy?" Joan asks her boss as the sheriff lugs his drone through the door in Friday Harbor.

"Very cool," Dave Anderson replies. "Easy to fly and it streams a live camera view back to me."

"Seriously, does this have any practical application to police work or are you just indulging your second childhood?"

"I think it does. I have a job in mind for it already."

"And it has enough range to do what you want?"

"Couple of miles," Anderson replies, "and about 25 minutes of flying time on a full charge. That's enough to provide a lot of information." He plugs the charger cord into the drone and the AC plug into a wall socket. "I'll be up and running again shortly."

*

"Dorothy, how do you feel?" Marie asks.

158

Dorothy blinks her eyes. "Huh?"

"How are you?"

"Uh . . .," she begins, propping herself on her side to face Marie. "I've . . . been better. A little woozy." Dorothy coughs once.

"Are you awake enough to talk?"

"I don't . . . know," she groans. "I'll try."

"Why did you jump?"

"Stupidity," Dorothy replies. She pauses before adding, "I felt cornered between you and Dutch."

"I'm sorry," Marie says. "Nothing is worth throwing your life away."

"I thought it was," Dorothy says. "I didn't think it through. That water really focuses the mind. I was so shocked I couldn't breathe. Then I gulped water."

Marie sits quietly, giving Dorothy a chance to continue when she's ready.

Dorothy adds, "By the way, where is he?"

"Dutch?" Marie asks.

"Yeah."

"Upstairs. He's asking to see you but this deck is closed to all but the crew."

"Can we just leave it that way for now?" Dorothy asks.

"Certainly. Was there something you wanted to say to us about the investigation?"

"We talked about a deal, is that right?"

Robert is sitting in the corner, but at this point he rises and comes to Dorothy's bedside. "If you'll give me something helpful, I'll ask the prosecutor to take it into consideration at sentencing. I can't imagine you'll avoid jail entirely, but it'll be a lot less time than you'd be looking at otherwise. Before we go further I need to read you your rights, and I'd like your permission to record this interview," he says, pulling a digital recorder from his shirt pocket and switching it on.

Robert recites the Miranda warning. Dorothy acknowledges she understands, and that she waives her right to an attorney.

"Then let's begin," Robert says. "Whose idea was it to throw that pilot, Bob Harlowe, overboard?"

"Dutch."

"Dutch ordered him killed?"

"I think so. I'm not sure," she says, waiving her arm dismissively. "Maybe the boys were just supposed to scare him, but I think Dutch wanted him off the payroll permanently, if you know what I mean."

"Why?"

"Well that's obvious. Bob was unhappy, very conflicted. We were afraid he was going to spill everything to Shane the next day. Said he had no idea what business we were really in till he met Dutch and realized what he was supposed to do."

"Which was?"

"Fly poachers in and out of bush camps. Transport illegal trophy kills and such."

"And this whole business with Nguyen?"

"He's our best customer."

"You've dealt with him before?"

"Oh yes, numerous times."

"And he was on the boat to receive a delivery?"

"Yes. He takes the raw ivory back to Washington to modify it and prepare false documents, and export it to Vietnam and I suppose China."

"Can you tell me his real name?"

"I don't know. We never discussed that. He operates with a slew of aliases and forged documents. Dutch calls him Nguyen but I have no idea what his actual name is."

"Where did he take the ivory for processing?"

"He's very secretive. Somewhere in Washington. I don't think he was planning to get off in Juneau and go by floatplane – that was a last-minute change when he got nervous. He never said where the plane was going. Dutch had to scramble to get a pilot and plane to Juneau on such short notice."

"Anything else?"

"If Dutch finds out I talked to you, I'm dead."

"We need you alive, Mrs. DeGroot," Robert says. "You'll have protection."

*

At the purser's desk, Dutch waves his arms.

"She's my wife, for god's sake. She nearly died. I don't understand this at all. Is she going to live?"

"I told you, sir, the captain's orders are for no visitors and no exceptions until she's out of danger. She is receiving 24-hour care from our EMTs and a doctor who happened to be among the passengers, but she nearly drowned and lost some body heat. Until she's fully stabilized, she needs complete rest. I'll let you know just as soon as it's possible for you to go to her side."

Nothing about this adds up, Dutch thinks. Why was she so depressed as to attempt suicide? Why is the crew keeping her isolated from him? Bellingham is 12 hours away. The boat can't get there fast enough now.

In the cafeteria, Shane, Brad, Irene, Robert and Marie sit around a large round table.

"The hours between now and Bellingham are critical," Robert says. "Dutch is totally isolated. He's lost everyone, his thugs, his wife. He's stuck on this boat now all the way to Bellingham. He knows we are hot after Nguyen. For the next 12 hours he's got nowhere to run. With so little control over his fate, not knowing why he's being kept away from Dorothy, he's unpredictable and dangerous, so be careful."

"Is there any chance he has a weapon?" Brad asks.

"Guns aren't allowed on the ferry but nobody screens luggage for them," Robert says. "We have to assume he might. It's not his style to take direct action that can be traced to him, but he's never been this tightly cornered before."

Brad is thinking how much has changed. Seven days ago he and Shane were slinking around the boat in disguise, unsure who they could trust. Now the whole team meets openly at a large table in the middle of the room.

"I know it's crazy," Marie says, "but I actually feel sorry for Mrs. DeGroot."

"I have a hard time feeling anything for her after the murders of Bob Harlowe and Bella," Brad says. There's that name again. He steals a glance at Irene. She keeps a poker face.

"I liked Bob," she says. "He didn't deserve what happened."

"Well, think about Dorothy," Marie remarks. "She's ruined and she did it to herself. She married Dutch for wealth and power – nothing else. She achieved both and they did not bring her happiness. The marriage was loveless. She threw away her life and that's sad – rather tragic. Turning against Dutch was her last, desperate play to come out of this with her life. It's no wonder she panicked and jumped overboard in a moment of despair."

"At least she still has a life," Robert says. "That's more than her victims. People make all kinds of excuses and rationalizations for what they do, give you the 'Poor me' story, but we're all responsible for ourselves. We all know when we've stepped outside the norms of society, the rules by which civilized people live."

Brad changes the subject. "Where do things stand in the search for Nguyen?"

Shane replies, "Dave Anderson is running down several leads and thinks he has an especially promising one on Orcas Island. We've got nothing so far in the surrounding counties, so San Juan County still looks like our best bet.

"This guy is like a ghost," Robert remarks. "Covers his tracks. He does everything with cash and fake identities."

"So what's next?" Irene asks.

"I'm headed for Friday Harbor the minute this boat ties up in Bellingham," Shane says.

"Count me in," Marie says. "I'm not going home till I lay hands on that ivory. I just wish I'd packed more clothes. I only brought what I expected to need for a couple of nights on the ferry."

Brad turns to Irene. "What about us? Are you ready to get onto a plane back to Boise?"

"No," she replies. "We're just getting to the good part. But I could use a Laundromat, too."

"Bolivar can hold it together at the ranch for a few more days," Brad says. "I've got a story to write and I'd like to find out how it ends."

Chapter 29
Bellingham

Shane is up three hours before arrival in Bellingham to pack and enjoy a last quiet hour in the cafeteria. Bellingham Bay is like glass this morning and the sky is blue. It's good to be home – feels like a year since he was last here. The scrunch of a metal chair sliding back from the table rouses him from his daydreams. It's Dutch DeGroot.

"Obviously, you're not going to allow me to see my wife," Dutch begins in the subdued voice of someone who is quietly resigned. "How is she?"

"She's fine. Comfortable."

"When will I see her again?"

"In court."

"I hope you won't make the mistake of trusting her account of things."

"If you think she gets something wrong, you'll have a chance to give us your version later."

"This has been one misunderstanding after another. I regret that we ever did business with that Nguyen guy. I had no idea what he was about."

"It will all get sorted out."

The vessel inches closer to the Bellingham Cruise Terminal, making a wide sweep to turn around end for end. Then it backs alongside the pier to moor stern first. The purser asks passengers over the intercom to remain in their cabins for a few more minutes until he gives the all clear to exit, so the crew may have full access to the main corridors.

At the stern, the passenger-loading ramp is winched into place and secured to the vessel. Four officers of the Whatcom County Sheriff's Department come aboard. The purser meets them and they proceed to Dutch DeGroot's cabin, where they knock. Dutch opens the door.

"I have to tell you there is a .38 caliber pistol in my back pocket," he announces.

"Freeze!" one of the officers commands. All four pull their sidearms and aim them at him in two-handed stances. "Freeze!" the first officer commands again. Dutch is confused, not sure what to do. Should he reach for his wallet? One wrong move and he knows they will empty their guns into him.

"Keep your hands where I can see them!" the officer screams in an adrenalin-fueled voice. "Do not move! Do not move! Do not reach for the gun! Raise your hands slowly to your head and interlock your fingers. Now!" he commands. "Do it NOW!" Dutch complies and the officer body-slams him against the wall. Dutch's hands come apart and the officer screams again, "Freeze!" Dutch is visibly shaking. "Jeesus," he says. "I don't know what to do. I'm trying to cooperate."

The three other officers rush Dutch and grab the gun from his pocket, jostling him hard to the floor, pinning both arms behind him. "I can't breathe," he yells. Nobody cares.

They lift Dutch awkwardly to his feet, handcuff him roughly behind his back, frisk him, and lead him out into the corridor. DeGroot walks ashore with his head down, except for a brief glance at the blue sky. His ribs hurt. A large, wet spot covers the front of his pants and extends part way down his left leg. No one is there to take pictures or shout questions.

The purser gives the all clear to passengers and they stream into the corridors pulling their luggage on wheels, unaware of what has just happened.

Shane is pretty sure he knows why they were delayed going ashore. "Anybody riding with me?" he asks over his shoulder as they inch forward in line to debark. "I'm in long-term parking right here at the terminal."

"Do you have room for us?" Robert asks on behalf of himself and Marie.

Shane smiles and gives the thumbs up.

"You go ahead," Brad says. "We're going to rent a car so we can look around the islands some while we're here. We'll see you in Friday Harbor."

As Shane hits the button to unlock his Honda Accord, he suggests, "Let's take the scenic way – through old Fairhaven onto Chuckanut Drive. It's a winding road, not as fast as the interstate, but it hugs the shoreline and it's such a pretty day, it would be a shame not to make the most of it while you're here. We're not far from Anacortes, where we'll catch the boat to Friday Harbor.

"I'm all for a pretty drive," Robert says, opening the front passenger door for Marie. Once she is seated he closes it and slips into the back seat.

"Everything's going to be pretty today," Shane assures them. "We'll take Chuckanut Drive to the Skagit Flats, then swing out to Anacortes. You'll love the entire ferry ride through the San Juan Islands."

"We've been on the ferry for a week," Robert says. "Don't you have something else for us?"

"Hush now," Marie admonishes him.

"Trust me," Shane adds.

"Well, it's nice to be back on Mother Earth for a little bit again," Robert remarks.

"For a few hours anyway," Shane replies. "You'll like the scenery this morning but you should come back during tulip season for a real thrill." He pulls out of the ferry terminal, clunks across the railroad tracks and heads uptown a few blocks into Fairhaven before turning right to follow the shoreline on Chuckanut Drive.

"Wow, great old Victorian architecture," Marie says. "I wish we had time to stop at that bookstore we just passed. I keep forgetting this isn't a vacation. We have a job to do and I'm starting to feel lucky."

*

In Friday Harbor, Dave Anderson ponders the next step. Everything he's learned so far points to the Hoang household as the likeliest destination for the powerboat that left Roche Harbor the other night. Security at the house is heavy and it's not the kind of place people just go knock on the door.

From Google Earth he can see the property has a boathouse large enough to accommodate the powerboat, though there's no boat in sight. It could be inside the building. The owner is new on Orcas within the last year and is doing a good job of staying invisible in the community.

In fact, the Hoang name has no history at all connected to this house – no children in school, no relatives, no voter registration, no spouse, no utility accounts, no social media, no previous addresses, and no registered boats or vehicles. It all contributes to his feeling that the owner of the house is hiding something.

Still, he needs more if he's going to ask for a search warrant.

Shane and his entourage are on the way and should arrive by mid afternoon. The sheriff promises Shane he will wait to confer once they arrive, and not make any moves in the meanwhile that will alert the owner. But when the time comes, he has some ideas.

*

"We've got some time," Shane tells his passengers. "Because of a midday gap in the ferry schedule, the next boat to Friday Harbor won't leave Anacortes till 2:40. So let's swing out to LaConner and play tourist, and then grab a bite of lunch in Anacortes before we head out to the ferry terminal."

It's a popular decision with Marie, who proclaims the historic village of LaConner "adorable." Robert heads for the boardwalk overlooking Swinomish Channel and watches a procession of work boats and yachts pass under the orange arch bridge that links the town to the reservation on the far side. He's fascinated by the tribal buildings and nets with their glass floats, piled along shore just across from town.

"It looks very native," he says. "Reminds me of home, but a lot bigger."

"You'll like Anacortes, too. It's not as quaint but extremely maritime. It's a working town focused around the fishing industry, and drydocks and shipbuilding. And there are oil refineries, and huge tankers coming and going."

In Anacortes they walk around the marina and study all the commercial boats before heading a few blocks west to Commercial Avenue, window-shopping the restaurant selection. They settle on Dad's Diner for what Robert calls the best meal of his life.

By 1 pm they have satisfied their tourist longings and are ready to get back to work. They drive five miles west to the large ferry terminal, buy their tickets and get their vehicle in line in the holding area. Their boat, the 144-car *MV Samish*, arrives and unloads vehicles from the

169

islands, and then the traffic director waves them aboard. Right on schedule at 2:40 the boat pulls away from the dock for the 55-minute run to Friday Harbor by way of Lopez and Orcas.

"This just gets better and better," Marie says as the boat winds among islands and headlands forested right to the water's edge. Around each new turn, another enchanting view appears – a narrow channel, a hidden beach or sandspit, maybe deer grazing on a hillside. They pass harbor seals bobbing toward them in the water and rocks that are covered with birds. Sailboats and private yachts share the marine traffic lanes with them.

Orcas Island, Shane explains, is shaped like a horseshoe with a large bay, called East Sound, in the center, nearly cutting the island in half. Eastsound (one word) also happens to be the name of the island's main commercial center, located in the middle where the two legs of the horseshoe come together.

"We'll likely be coming back to Orcas from Friday Harbor and spending some time on the far side of the easterly leg of the horseshoe, since that's where the sheriff believes the ivory has been taken," he says.

Robert can smell the evergreens as the ferry weaves among islands, headlands and outcroppings that are densely forested, and he wonders what special challenges they will face if their suspect resists arrest or attempts to flee. Maybe the local sheriff has some experience dealing with this terrain. He now understands why it was so hard to predict where a powerboat was headed at night in these waters, running with no lights. He also understands why a powerboat of one's own is the way to get somewhere fast in these islands.

The ferry makes a quick stop at Lopez Island, then continues on to Orcas Landing, where there's a much larger cluster of buildings including a hotel, store and restaurant. But nothing prepares Robert and Marie for Friday Harbor, where an entire town sprawls upslope from the ferry landing and hundreds of boats are moored to piers and floats in the harbor.

They drive a short distance to the sheriff's office, where Brad and Irene are just parking their rental car. Sheriff Anderson steps out to the street to welcome his visitors. They all shake hands and he leads the entourage inside to a conference table.

"I think there's still some coffee in the pot if you're desperate enough," he remarks, gesturing to a half-filled carafe of black sludge in the corner. Everyone looks at each other and declines.

"I didn't think so," he continues. "The Bean Café is a better bet."

Shane explains that he and Anderson have been friends for years. "The sheriff is a Renaissance man," Shane says, "former veterinarian, former state legislator, former commercial fisherman, now county sheriff."

"That's a lot of hats," Brad remarks.

The sheriff remarks, "Maybe in my next life I'll become a writer. Shane and I worked together on some oil spill legislation a few years ago. With all these tankers and barges going through the islands, it's only a matter of time till something really catastrophic happens. If I can do something to help reduce the risk of a spill, I think I owe it to the next generation."

He outlines the reasons he believes the Hoang estate on the east side of Orcas Island is the likely whereabouts of the Vietnamese subject from the Alaska Ferry who has the walrus ivory. He also explains that he has insufficient grounds to request a search warrant. "We haven't even connected the boat to that property, except in the most circumstantial way."

He continues, "We need something stronger if we're going to enter and search the grounds," he says.

"Several of us saw the guy on the ferry and would recognize him if we saw him again," Shane says. "But I'll bet he rarely sets foot off the property."

"I have a sketch of him in my book," Irene adds, flipping pages in her sketch pad till she finds the right one.

"That's darn good," Shane says. "That's the guy I remember from the boat."

The sheriff jumps in. "I have a way for us to look around some without going up to the gate and introducing ourselves," the sheriff says. "It involves some risks, but might give us a preview of what we're getting into."

Chapter 30
Orcas Island

In a grassy clearing several hundred yards from the Hoang estate, the sheriff and two deputies unload the drone. Shane, Robert, Marie, Brad and Irene watch. They all arrive here in civilian attire in private vehicles to avoid attracting attention.

"Now this is high tech," Brad remarks as he looks over the machine. "Irene, don't you think we should have one of these for the ranch?"

"For Bolivar?" Irene deadpans.

"No, for me."

"Let me get back to you on that."

"It's remarkably easy to fly," Anderson comments. "And it's pretty small and surprisingly quiet, which are two more big points in its favor."

Moments later, the contraption lifts off with a soft whine. Anderson flies it straight up till it's hard to see against the blue sky, rotates it till he finds the beach on the video display, then begins following the shoreline toward the Hoang estate.

"We should have about 25 minutes of flying time," Anderson says, "but I'll play it safe and bring it back in 15." Moments later, the view on the video display opens up as the drone arrives over the house.

"I'll try to hover with the sun behind the drone so it'll be harder for people in the house to see anything if they happen to hear a strange sound," he says.

"Can you zoom in with that camera?" Robert asks.

The sheriff adjusts the camera control to give them a closer look at the deck, driveway and outbuildings. The yard is surprisingly devoid of human touches – no evidence of a garden, outdoor furniture, hammocks, barbecue equipment, lawn games or other typical touches of the leisure living. He rotates the camera to reveal several parked vehicles in the yard, including a Humvee and a black Jaguar.

"Nice car," Robert remarks. "Judging by the number of vehicles I think we can assume there may be about half-a-dozen people on the premises."

Shane studies the view. "Can you fly that thing low and steady?" he asks the sheriff.

"Up to a point. I'm new at this, you know."

"I think we need a look inside that boathouse," Shane says. "Could you pop it in there?"

"Jeesus, Shane. I'll try."

The sheriff flies the drone some distance offshore, then descends to a few feet off the water. The craft wobbles and he nearly dumps it into the water before he gets it lined up on the boathouse and begins flying toward it. It would not take much to miscalculate, he thinks. At this elevation, just above the ripples on the water, the view through the camera feels as if the device were screaming across the water, when in fact it is moving only a few miles per hour. The sheriff concentrates hard on keeping it steady. From some distance out, the stern of a boat is visible inside the structure up ahead.

"That's what I want to see," Shane declares, leaning closer to the video monitor.

The machine ducks inside the door to reveal a fancy, inboard powerboat. The sheriff hovers the device and pans for a view of the entire boat. It has a large inboard engine and a roomy cockpit, and probably several berths below deck.

Shane studies the pictures. "That fits the description of the boat several people said they saw leaving Roche Harbor."

"Holy crap!" Anderson yells.

A young man emerges from below decks and turns toward the drone. His face fills the camera and he's momentarily stunned. The sheriff throws the drone into reverse and backs out of the boathouse as the man pulls a handgun from his belt and runs from the building toward the house.

"Ok, now we've got a problem," the sheriff says. "They know we're watching."

"Except," Marie says, "they don't know who *we* are."

Shane interjects, "Can you set up a blockade right away on the driveway and figure out some way to bottle up that powerboat?"

"I'm on it," the sheriff replies. "But we don't have deep reserves to draw from and the powerboat is a real problem."

"Let me use your radio," Shane urges. He calls his office in Bellingham to request the Whatcom County Marine Unit. He also calls Skagit County to request any available Skagit watercraft based at Anacortes Marina. Anderson calls for his own marine unit, which at the moment is a long distance away at English Bay on San Juan Island.

"We're in luck," Shane says. "The Skagit boat is in Guemes Channel, only a few minutes away."

Robert Yuka interjects, "Hover where we can watch the house for a few minutes if we've got a little flying time left." Men disperse in several directions, apparently all armed.

"This is going to be messy," Shane sighs.

The drone ascends to an altitude of about 200 feet, just offshore.

"That's it, right there," Robert says.

On the deck of the house three men with handguns and binoculars scan the sky. One steps back inside and comes out with a rifle, and seems to be trying to get a fix on the object. The rifle jumps against the man's shoulder.

"That's a shot," Anderson announces, putting the drone into a dive, adding speed and losing the video.

By the estate's gated entrance, two San Juan County Sheriffs vehicles take up positions. Deputies string "Police line" tape across the nearby roadway. Back in the grassy clearing, the little drone appears over the treetops and the sheriff guides it to a controlled landing.

"What's the best way to approach the house on foot?" Marie asks.

"Are you sure you want to do that?" Anderson replies. "We'll have some backup in an hour or so."

"The longer we wait, the more time they have to hide the ivory and plan their next move. I want Nguyen, or whomever he calls himself, alive."

Anderson points out, "The whole property is fenced with chain link, but you can hike in on the beach. Unfortunately, there isn't much cover when you get closer."

Robert announces he will go with her. "I feel safer with you," he tells Marie.

"Awwww, aren't you a sweetheart?" Marie declares. They pin on their badges and sidearms.

"For the record I officially appoint both of you interim deputies of the San Juan County Sheriff's Office," Anderson says, handing them a walkie talkie. The two start hiking toward the beach. The sheriff loads up the drone in his vehicle and announces he will head for the roadblock at the driveway entrance and establish his command post there.

"Let's see if we can create a distraction by the gate," he says. "If we're lucky they might even let us enter the property without a warrant."

"I'm not optimistic of that," Shane remarks. Brad, Shane and Irene go with the sheriff.

At the property gate, she sheriff speaks into the intercom and requests permission to enter. For several minutes there is no answer – then an Asian voice comes over the speaker.

"What is it, sheriff?"

"We're investigating some illegal activity on the island," the sheriff says. "I'd like to come in and talk – make sure everything's ok."

"Everything is ok here," comes the reply. "We have very fine security." The sheriff notices for the first time a webcam mounted near the gate and wonders how many others there may be. People in the house are watching him – he's sure of that. He knows there are at least three men with guns on the property. If he can keep them focused on him it might help Robert and Marie.

Down on the beach, the walking is difficult. The high tide laps at the rocks in places, so that Robert and Marie have to climb over boulders, drift logs and living trees that have tipped over nearly horizontal to the ground.

"Sir, are you the property owner?" the sheriff asks over the intercom at the gate.

"I am his representative," comes the disembodied voice on the speaker.

"May I ask what is the owner's name?"

A long delay follows. The speaker seems to have been turned off. Then it crackles with static as it is turned back on.

"Nguyen," comes the reply.

"I thought it was Hoang," the sheriff replies.

The speaker goes silent again for half-a-minute, then crackles to life with static.

"One is an affectionate nickname and the other is the family name," comes the reply.

The answer strikes the sheriff as doubletalk. "I'd really like to speak with him," Anderson replies. "And while I've got you here, may I ask your name please?" He's trying to keep the guy tied up as long as possible, along with any others who are following all this with him.

"Phan."

"Mr. Phan, would you please buzz me in so I may talk with Mr. Hoang?"

Another long delay.

"Mr. Hoang values his privacy, and he's feeling a bit under the weather today. He suggests you make an appointment for another time, perhaps."

On the beach, Robert and Marie are plastered behind a rock two hundred feet from the house, reconnoitering. From this point onward they'll be in the open.

"See it?" Robert asks. "On the boathouse roof."

Marie looks where Robert is pointing. It's a webcam that pans back and forth across the property every 30 seconds. The house is built into a slope that leads down to the boathouse. The camera would give a clear view of anyone crossing that lawn. The deck and living area are upstairs, with a commanding view of the water. The lower level appears to be a separate unit, a mother-in-law apartment or daylight basement.

"If we wait till the camera passes and then make a dash, I think we can get to the side of the house before the camera pans back," he says.

"And then what?" Marie asks.

Just then the boulder by Robert's cheek explodes in a cloud of rock chips and dust. A second shot sends him spinning and he sinks to the ground. A third shot rips into Marie's backpack. She crouches and returns fire in a burst of five shots.

"Robert! Oh god, no! Don't do this to me! Robert! " A large circle of blood spreads rapidly from his upper arm. Marie pulls him behind a rock and unclips the walkie-talkie from his belt.

"Officer down! Officer down," she cries. "We're 200 feet from the house, taking fire on the beach."

"Roger," the sheriff responds. "We're coming in right now."

Marie tears off her backpack and then her shirt, and fashions a tourniquet to slow the bleeding from Robert's arm. "Stay with me," she cries.

"Don't be dramatic," he mumbles in a weak voice.

Now that the occupants of the property have opened fire, the sheriff, accompanied by Shane and another deputy, have all the reason they need to enter. They back a patrol car to the gate, climb up on the car's roof and lower themselves across the fence.

The minute their boots hit the ground, they take fire from an unseen shooter. They disperse behind trees and fire back. The sheriff fires a shot that brings down the gunman, and they move forward cautiously.

On the beach, Marie concentrates on staying low. Bullets strike the rocks and trees all around her position, pinning her. She hears the sound she's been dreading – the engine of the powerboat starting. She sneaks a look toward the boathouse. The powerboat is backing out in a cloud of blue exhaust, but she sees something else that raises her spirits.

In front of the boathouse, the Skagit County Sheriff's marine unit approaches behind a cloud of spray from its water canon. It hoses down the powerboat with a large stream from the nozzle on its bow. Three deputies with the marine unit aim rifles toward the powerboat and a voice on the bullhorn advises, "Turn off your engine, lay down your weapons immediately and stand topside with your hands behind your heads."

Two men emerge from the cockpit and put down their weapons. A moment later, a third appears wearing a top hat and dark glasses, water draining from his pants and sleeves. Even from this distance, Marie recognizes him as the mercurial Mr. Nguyen from the Alaska Ferry.

Bingo.

As the sheriff, Shane and another deputy come up the driveway, Marie waves her arms. Shane breaks away from the others and rushes toward her as the sheriff and his deputy approach the house. An individual on the deck of the house puts down his rifle and places his hands behind his head.

"Orcas Fire and Rescue will be here in a minute," Shane says as he reaches Marie. "A chopper is also on the way to fly Robert to Anacortes."

The marine unit throws a line to the powerboat's crew and instructs them to make it fast to the bow. Officers tow the vessel to the beach, where Mr. Nguyen and his associates wade ashore. Sheriff Anderson searches and handcuffs the suspects, and sits them down on the lawn to wait.

Medics arrive and set up an I.V. for Robert. He looks better and jokes with them. Marie and Shane rejoin the sheriff's men. Deputies search the house for additional shooters and declare the premises clear for them to go room to room. Someone hands Marie a shirt from the house. "They won't miss it," he says.

Marie and Shane enter the house from the deck. "I could get used to this lifestyle," Shane says, looking around the luxurious living room and den. A large telescope points out the windows at the water. Marie makes a sweep of the main floor, then leads Shane downstairs to the lower level.

"Well this is more like it," she says as she gets her first look at the room. "Just look at this. It's a complete lab."

Spread out in front of her are several tables piled with walrus tusks, skulls and baculums. She finds saws, carving knives, brushes, dyes and engraving tools. Finished pieces from an earlier hunt are stored in bins awaiting buyers. Also nearby are cartons and packing materials, foam pellets, bubble wrap and strapping tape to prepare packages for shipment.

She points out to Shane several work stations for artists. Marie photographs it all and dictates extensive notes into a digital recorder. In Hoang's office on the main floor she finds video monitors for the security webcams and, more importantly, journals of handwritten sales records for ivory artifacts, with names and addresses of the buyers.

Nguyen, or Hoang, apparently is old school – likes to keep ledgers. Brad and Irene join them.

"So this is what it was all about," Brad remarks. "A lot of people went to a lot of trouble to make a few dollars the illegal way."

"This is just what we need to put Nguyen away for a long time and tie a bow on our case against the DeGroots," Marie tells the others. Out on the lawn, Nguyen sits in his top hat and dark glasses, staring straight ahead.

*

"You were lucky," the doctor assures Robert as a nurse wheels him out of Emergency at Island Hospital in Anacortes. His right arm is wrapped in a sling. "The bullet didn't break any bones, just made you bleed. You're good to go, with a couple of follow-ups with an MD. Get these prescriptions filled right away for pain killers and antibiotics."

The nurse adds, "It would have been more serious if someone hadn't stopped the bleeding when they did."

"That was my guardian angel," Robert remarks.

Shane, Marie, Brad and Irene wait by the curb.

"Thank you for the shirt," Robert says to Marie, holding up a plastic bag with something bloody in it. "I am quite fond of it."

"That is beyond repulsive," she replies with a grimace. "I'll get you another but first I'd like to get you home to bed."

"I like how your mind works," Robert remarks.

"What did you say?"

"Just blathering. I said that's very kind. But I can look after myself, you know."

"We'll discuss it in the morning."

"By the way, where is home?"

"Motel 6."

"I never heard what you found in the house?"

182

Marie grins. "We nailed 'em, Bobby. It was all there. Absolutely everything."

"Bobby?"

*

In an interview room at the Whatcom County jail, Shane and Marie break the news to Dutch DeGroot that they have Nguyen behind bars and they recovered the ivory. They have his personal ledgers of other transactions and payments he's made to DeGroot, and records of his dealings with buyers of ivory in Asia. They're still not quite sure of his real name. The case is now very strong against Dorothy and Dutch for brokering the walrus hunt, as is the case for the murder of pilot Bob Harlowe.

"He's a slippery guy," Dutch says of Nguyen. "I wasn't sure you would find him."

Marie adds, "The story was big news all over Alaska. We even got a lucky break. The pilot who flew Nguyen to Roche Harbor read about the bust in the *Juneau Empire* and decided to come forward. He filled us in on some other charters he's flown for you."

Dutch sighs. "When it rains, it pours."

"There is one thing you could do for us," Marie says. "Just to make a clean breast of things."

"And that is?"

"Tell me how to find those walrus hunters. You won't be doing business with them again in this lifetime."

"They live somewhere outside Nenana. I always reached them on the pay phone at the bar in town."

"Names?"

"Big Don and Junior. Those are the only names I ever had for them. We did everything in cash."

Shane excuses himself to go make a phone call. He steps outside and punches numbers on his cell phone.

"Billy?" he says. "I told you I'd let you know how things turned out. We got 'em. We got those guys."

"Are they going to jail?"

"Every last one of them."

"Way to go, Dad."

*

Marie passes the information about the hunters to her Fairbanks office to follow up. Two such local celebrities shouldn't be hard to find in a bar in Nenana. Once they're in custody, positive identification should be easy with the help of Paul Fisher, the pilot who flew them from Platinum to Haines and tipped her office that something was suspicious about those guys.

Fisher also gives them a lead on the "regular guy" who was originally scheduled to fly the hunters from Platinum to Haines. Marie calls the state troopers and asks them to detain him for questioning about this and other illegal hunts.

The Two Rivers musher, Hank Hickok, also got a good look at the hunters when they transferred the bags to his truck at the Haines Airport. He'll be called to testify against them.

*

"Is that it?" Irene remarks. "Is our work here done?"

"I think it is," Brad replies. "Except for the story I need to write when we get home."

"Better you than me. Where do you start on something like this?"

"I guess with one small detail. That's how most big stories start."

"There is someone I'd like to see before we get on the plane back to Boise," Irene says. "It's on our way to the airport."

*

Irene pushes the doorbell. Somewhere inside, chimes ring *ding-dong*. A dog barks once and she hears someone cross the room to the door. It opens to reveal a pretty brunette in her 20s, in sweats. Irene can see the sibling resemblance.

"Elizabeth?" Irene asks.

"Yes. You must be Irene and Brad, the people who called. Excuse me just a second," she pleads, turning back to the little terrier. "Moose, go to your mat," she commands, and the dog runs across the room to its bed. She invites Brad and Irene into the living room and gestures to the sofa.

"Moose?" Brad asks. "That's a big name."

"My brother got him for me and gave him the big-hearted name. May I offer you coffee or tea?"

"No, thank you," Irene begins. "We can only stay a moment on our way to the airport. I wanted to tell you in person how sorry I am about your brother. He was our fellow passenger for a few days on the Alaska Ferry."

"You were the last person to talk with him?" Elizabeth asks.

"I believe I was. I got to know him a little, a sensitive man, and I felt we connected a bit."

"That's Robert," Elizabeth smiles. "A sensitive soul and a genuinely decent man. He just wanted to fly and I guess he hooked up with the wrong people."

"He realized that and was trying to do something about it," Irene says. She gives Elizabeth the background of Robert's final days, his conflict with his boss and the telephone tip that led Detective Shane Lindstrom to be on the same ferry with him.

"How did you get involved in all this?" she asks.

"That's quite a story," Brad explains. Shane, the detective, and I pursued these people two years ago in connection with the death of a journalism classmate of mine from the university. We just couldn't quite put them away at that time. It was pure coincidence that Irene and I ended up on the same boat with them last week to Alaska and got another chance to do it."

Irene picks up the story. "Brad and Shane needed someone to keep an eye on the DeGroots that they wouldn't recognize. That sounded like something I could do without attracting too much attention, because of my sketching, so I took that on."

She continues, "Your brother was ready to talk with the police. I told him I'd arrange it the next day, but there was no next day. I blame myself for his death. I wish I could go back and do something differently."

"It's not your fault," Elizabeth says. "No one could foresee what happened. It means a lot to me that you looked me up."

"The night your brother died, we talked in the ship's bar. He asked me to sketch him so our conversation wouldn't attract suspicion. I thought you should have the sketch," she says, handing Elizabeth the page from her sketch pad. Brad notices a tear roll down Elizabeth's cheek, and no one speaks for a moment.

"That's my brother," Elizabeth says. This will be very special to me — a last memory of Bob that I will treasure." She stands and reaches out her arms to Irene, and they hug.

"Miss Harlowe," Brad begins, "we'd love to have you be our guest in Idaho whenever you feel like a change of scenery. Come and see us. Bring Moose and a friend if you like. Our ranch is a good place to relax and enjoy the beauty of the rivers and mountains, and clear the mind."

Thinking maybe he hasn't laid it on thick enough, Brad continues. "Irene will take you horseback riding. Bolivar, our Basque foreman, will take you to the Mountain Village Restaurant for a cinnamon roll as big as your head. He has an eye for the pretty women and a good, home-baked treat."

"That all sounds really tempting to me right now," Elizabeth says. "Every bit of it."

"We'll look forward to your visit. I think it would make your brother happy to know he introduced us. We've all suffered losses here. It's time to take a bad thing and make something good, new and positive out of it," Brad says. "That's all any of us can do, and what we have to do."

Chapter 31
Stanley, Idaho

Brad Haraldsen sits on the deck of his Stanley, Idaho, ranch, looking down at the lush green floor of the Stanley Basin river bottom. The sky is cloudless this morning and the Sawtooth Peaks reach like white teeth into the deep, blue sky. The Salmon River tumbles noisily through the valley, bank full with spring runoff. Patches of snow still dot the landscape.

He types a few words on his laptop, then takes a break to lavish attention on Bear and Idaho. He massages the shoulders of each dog, working his way toward the rump, their favorite part. In turn, they lean into him. "Missed you guys up there in Alaska," he says. "It's good to be home." Ida licks his hand. Brad wishes he could tell her they finally got the people who killed Bella.

Irene backs through the screen door with two mugs of coffee. She hands one to Brad and sits down with the other in a wicker chair nearby.

"Well that was fun," she says, taking a sip.

"What? Alaska?"

"Yeah. And your friends. Those are some nice people – Shane, Robert and Marie. I see why you like working with Shane."

"I was just thinking . . ." Brad begins.

"What?"

"I wonder if that sheriff, Dave Anderson, ever told his wife about the drone."

Irene smiles. "How's the story coming?"

"It's a big topic. Michener gave Alaska everything he had. I'm a little daunted by that."

"Nothing daunts you. Let me know if you want to do so some more research. I'll clear my schedule."

"I think we'll be going back for Robert and Marie's wedding."

"There's a wedding?"

"There will be," Brad assures her. "I can sense it. By the way have you seen Bolivar today?"

"He's running an errand in Stanley."

"I'll bet. To the Mountain Village Restaurant?"

"Probably," Irene says. "Danielle's working the breakfast shift. I'll let you write. I have book club today and need to think about my report."

Brad stares at his screen.

It started with a telephone tip, he types. *Before it was over, it grew to involve 18 dead Alaska walruses, several airplanes, one dead pilot, six police agencies, two state ferries, one gunfight and a basement lab where raw ivory would have become tourist trinkets for the Asian market.*

His heart isn't in it. A call on his cell phone interrupts him. It's Shane.

The news should shock him but it doesn't. Dorothy committed

suicide last night in the Bellingham jail. Shane tells him she hanged herself. The jailer found her on his rounds at 2 a.m. She tied bed sheets together – a very poor system that probably was slow and basically strangled her. Brad shivers at the thought.

Shane says she left no note. She was not on suicide watch – was considered low risk because she was a witness turned state's evidence, facing the prospect of a lighter sentence for her crimes. But hindsight is always clearer and it's obvious now that she should have been.

Shane adds a personal note. "Tell Irene that Dorothy had her sketch on the wall of her cell. It was the only personal item she displayed."

Marie is right. After everything, Dorothy is a lonely and tragic figure – a woman of charm and ability who grew up in poverty and spent her whole life looking for financial security at any cost. She sought it through political power and a marriage of convenience with Dutch. In the end, neither of those brought what she wanted – the simple joy that lights the lives of people like Robert and Marie. The future for Dorothy was unbearable.

For Brad, Dorothy's death and Dutch's arrest bring closure on Bella's death, but it isn't satisfying. Bella and the young pilot, Bob Harlowe, died only because they got in the way of desperate people. Brad and Irene can still make a life because it wasn't their time. Irene survived a close call on the ferry when those bikers slammed into her. That is the randomness of life. Luck calls the shots – some of it good and some bad.

A long life brings many joys and a few regrets. Deeply in love with Bella when they were undergraduates at the university, Brad briefly experienced the absolute high of winning her trust. But geography soon intervened. Brad fumbled his chances with her repeatedly. Yet over a lifetime she remained a comet in his universe, returning every few years for another pass.

Her reappearances always thrilled him. He wondered what his life might have been if he'd gotten it right with her. In a moment of uncommon clarity he realizes it might not have been as good as the life he has right now.

He is happy for Robert and Marie, two adventurous spirits who seem perfect for each other. They got their man. He is happy for Shane, who enjoys the unconditional love and admiration of a 10-year-old son. He is happy for Sheriff Dave Anderson, who got the win he needed with that darned drone. Now the sheriff can retire fulfilled and write books, reinvent himself yet again.

He is happy for himself and Irene, who seem to have found their way forward after some tough years in their marriage. He is even happy for his ranch foreman Bolivar, chasing a young man's fantasy at the Mountain Village Restaurant. More power to him.

Brad realizes he can't help it. He likes writing happy stories. Two smiling dogs look up at him. Who wouldn't be happy?

He feels the spark of something reawakening in his life.

From *Final Deception:*
A Whidbey Island Mystery
Available from Amazon.com and Whidbey Island bookstores

In the blackness, Bella Morelli pitched face forward in an ungainly dive, wind roaring in her ears. The four seconds took forever and she had two last thoughts – surprise and dread. She hit the water all wrong like a breaching whale, lungs first, a horrible impact, and that was the last she felt.

*

Deception Pass Bridge connects Washington's Fidalgo and Whidbey islands across a deep chasm. It is 180 feet from the bridge deck to the water, depending on tide. From there it's 130 more in icy darkness to the bottom.

A young person in peak condition, hitting the water feet first in perfect form, can survive if they miss the rocks and regain the surface before drowning or hypothermia. A 67-year-old cannot. Whirlpools and eddies reach out to clutch and pull them down.

From *Louis and Fanny:*
15 Years on the Alaska Frontier
Available from Amazon.com and Whidbey Island bookstores

Trees sagged under a blanket of white. Boots kicked up powder in the Streets of Seward, Alaska, as the mail steamer *Dora* pulled away from the dock. The ship trailed a plume of black smoke. Captain C.B. McMullen stood at the stern, taking a last look at civilization and pondering what he'd find on his return to Kodiak.

He'd just reached Seward with a firsthand account of conditions in the remote outpost of Kodiak. Mt. Katmai had exploded 100 miles from Kodiak in a volcanic eruption that was still spewing ash into the atmosphere. The *Dora* had called on Kodiak after tense hours sailing blind in conditions that could have cost McMullen the ship and all aboard.

Now he was going back with the minister's wife.

FINAL PASSAGE

ABOUT THE AUTHOR

Dan Pedersen grew up in Western Washington and now makes his home on Whidbey Island with his wife, Sue, and their adventurous canine, Duncan. He received two journalism degrees from the University of Washington in the 1960s and 70s, served in the US Air Force and went on to become a reporter and editor for several newspapers in Idaho and Washington, including a large outdoor weekly. He also managed a magazine and other publications for an insurance and financial services corporation.

Alaska is part of the family culture. His father spent his boyhood in Douglas, Seward and Skagway. Pedersen Glacier, near Seward, is named for his grandfather. The author's book, *Louis & Fanny: 15 Years on the Alaska Frontier*, tells his family's story.

He is the author of several books, many short stories and a weekly blog about nature and rural living, Dan's Blog. This is his second mystery, the sequel to *Final Deception: A Whidbey Island Mystery*.

Made in the USA
Columbia, SC
07 August 2017